MORE THAN ONE WAY TO SKIN A CAT

They circled each other warily at first. Pike was in no hurry to die, and he had no intention of rushing in until he had studied the Indian for a while.

As it turned out, Walking Cat did not have much patience. He slashed at Pike again and again, each time coming closer. Pike moved back just enough to avoid the blade and timed the Indian's thrusts. When he finally thought he had the man figured out, he stepped forward quickly, caught the brave's arm, turned it, and brought the handle of his own knife down on Walking Cat's elbow. Sweat broke out on the Indian's brow, and Pike was sure that it was a result of having his arm broken.

With his left hand, the brave plucked the knife from the nerveless fingers of his right. His arm hanging useless at his side, Walking Cat continued to stalk Pike, holding the knife ready in his left hand.

Suddenly Pike tossed his own knife aside. The Indian straightened up and stared at Pike in confusion.

"Come on, Walking Cat," Pike said, waving the brave closer, "let's get this over with. I've got more important things to do."

Just as he had hoped, Pike had so humiliated the Indian that Walking Cat threw caution to the wind and charged him, the knife leveled at the big mountain man's heart . . .

MOUNTAIN JACK PIKE

#7: THE RUSSIAN BEAR

JOSEPH MEEK

PINNACLE BOOKS
WINDSOR PUBLISHING CORP.

PINNACLE BOOKS

are published by

Windsor Publishing Corp.
475 Park Avenue South
New York, NY 10016

First Printing: January, 1991

Printed in the United States of America

Prologue

Ivan Koloff was not called "the Russian Bear" for nothing. He was a huge, bearlike man with a hairy chest, wide, sloping shoulders, and treetrunk legs. His arms were not musclebound, but many a man had been crushed—a few to death—within the circle of those hairy arms.

The woman inside those arms now, though, was in no danger of being crushed. Her name was Vanya Ivoroff. She was a big woman, standing about five-eight when she was standing. At the moment, however, she was lying in a tent with Koloff, a bearskin pulled over them. His large hands were caressing her big round breasts and his mouth roamed over her neck and shoulders.

Abruptly, Koloff raised himself on his hands and knees and then lowered himself onto her. When his rigid penis, itself like a tree trunk, penetrated her she gasped, wrapping her arms and legs around him. They stayed like that, he pumping in and out of her and she holding on for dear life, until they both groaned and shouted, the sound echoing through the emptiness outside.

While Vanya slept Ivan Koloff rose and wrapped another bearskin around him. Thus clad, he left the tent and stared up at the mountains. They were called the Rocky Mountains, and he had come here all the way from Russia not only to see them but to hunt in them as well.

There was another reason Koloff was called the Russian Bear. Though he hunted many animals, bears were his specialty. In his own country, Ivan Koloff was considered a great hero, but Ivan did not think of himself as heroic. He did, however, consider himself the greatest hunter in the world, and he had come to the United States to prove that over ten months ago. Since then he had hunted the American mountain lion and the Plains buffalo, he had even tried his hand at shooting rabbit. Now, finally, he was after the American brown bear.

Ivan had not come to America alone. Around his tent four others were pitched. One of them was Vanya's. Another belonged to Colonel Uri Makarov, Koloff's bodyguard. The Russian government did not want their great hero coming to harm in a foreign country.

The third tent lodged Charles Severance. If he had a rank, it had not been revealed to Koloff, but he was a representative of the American government. It was his job too to see that Koloff came to no harm.

Koloff found it ironic that someone believed that a hunter such as himself needed not one but two bodyguards.

In the fourth tent were four men Koloff had brought with him. They carried his equipment, saw to it that his guns were always in working order, flushed his prey, and generally took care of such menial tasks as cooking.

One of these men, Leonid, was bent over the fire now, preparing a pot of coffee. Today was the day they would begin to ascend the Rocky Mountains. Koloff was looking forward not only to encountering the bear he sought but also to meeting some of the mountain men he had heard so much about.

Stepping toward the fire, Ivan pulled the bearskin tightly around him, then on a whim simply let it drop.

Leonid looked up at that moment but showed no surprise. Nothing that Ivan Koloff did ever surprised Leonid or any of the other men who had been with him for years. Leonid marveled, however, as he always did, at the amount of hair that covered his master's body. Leonid did not know how women could share a bed with such a hairy brute, but then, maybe women liked that . . .

Of course, Koloff had no problem finding women to sleep with him. Most women dreamed of sleeping with a legend like the great Koloff. So why had Koloff decided to bring Vanya to America with him? Could it be that after countless women, he had finally found one he wanted to keep?

Leonid poured a mug of coffee and carried it to the nude Koloff.

"Thank you, Leonid."

"Da," Leonid said, then corrected himself, "Yes, you are welcome."

It was Koloff's wish that they all speak English while they were in America.

"Your English is getting better, my friend."

Leonid nodded and went back to the fire.

Koloff sipped the coffee. The heat of it seared his insides.

"Ivan . . ." Vanya's voice called from inside the tent.

"In a moment," he called back. He wanted to finish his coffee while looking at the mountains.

Ivan was eager to meet one of the famed mountain men he had heard so much about — Jim Bridger, Kit Carson, or perhaps even Jack Pike. He had heard that Pike was a mountain of a man and that he had never been bested in physical combat by man or beast.

Koloff tossed Leonid the empty cup and wondered idly if Pike had ever wrestled a bear.

He turned and went back into the tent. Vanya was on her knees, waiting for him. Her black hair hung to her waist, and her breasts were pale, like the moon at night. As he approached her, he watched her dark brown nipples

7

harden.

Vanya reached out to touch him, then pulled her hands back.

"You are cold."

He went to his knees and pulled her close.

"And you are burning!"

"Oh," she said, shivering from the cold of him. Between them his penis thickened. Her nipples were so hard they scraped his chest. He reached behind her and cupped her big buttocks, squeezing them so tightly that he left the imprint of his fingers on her flesh.

She reached behind him and tried to do the same, but his buttocks were as hard as stone. Instead, she drew her nails over them and moaned as his mouth moved over her shoulders.

Quickly, his body warmed, and she pushed him down on his back and straddled him, taking him inside of her again.

"We go up into the mountains today, do we not?" she asked.

"We do," he said, gripping her hips as she moved on him.

"And you will look for your bear?"

"That is right."

"And after that?"

"What do you mean, after that?"

"When will we go home?" she asked. "I miss the motherland."

It was odd, but Koloff did not.

"I do not know when we will go home."

"But after your bear—"

"After the bear," he said, "perhaps I will find something else to hunt."

"What?"

"Something new," he said, "something I've never hunted before."

"Like wha—ohhh!"

He lifted his hips, driving himself deeply into her, and

she gasped and threw her head back.

Koloff had an idea what his new prey might be, but he wasn't mentioning it to anyone.

Not yet.

Part One
The Meeting

Chapter One

Pike tried to move his hands, but they were tied too tightly. He looked over at his friend, Skins McConnell, who was having the same problem. Both were standing with their backs to a tree, hands and legs tied. Actually, their hands weren't tied *to* the tree so much as *around* it.

"This will teach you to insult a Crow Indian," Pike said to McConnell.

"Me?" McConnell said. "I thought it was you who insulted them."

"I'm not the one who tried to make off with their leader's squaw."

"How was I supposed to know she was his squaw?" McConnell said.

"Yeah, well, tell him that."

"I did tell him that," McConnell said. "He just didn't believe me."

"So now we just wait to see what they're gonna do to us," Pike said. "You know, I had other plans for the rest of my life, Skins."

"And I didn't?"

Pike shook his head and looked around. Crow braves were hunkered down all around them, watching them carefully. Even if he got his hands free, where was he going to go? They'd be on him in seconds.

13

No, there was nothing more they could do at this point, nothing but wait for Walking Cat to decide how he wanted to kill them.

"Besides," McConnell said, "she only wanted to come with me because of you."

"Of me?"

"Yeah," McConnell said, "she didn't want me, she wanted you."

"You should have told her she couldn't have either one of us."

"I did."

From where they were they could see the squaw in question. She was standing against a tree of her own, watching the two of them.

"Look at her," McConnell said. "Could you say no to her?"

Pike looked. She was tall for an Indian, and full-bodied. Her breasts were straining against her clothes, and her calves were full and firm.

"Yeah," Pike said finally, "if my life depended on it, yeah, I could."

McConnell hesitated, then said, "Well, that's the difference between you and me, Pike . . . you got more willpower."

Pike was about to answer when he saw a group of braves approaching. Tagging along behind them was the squaw. In the center of the group was Walking Cat, their leader.

When the braves reached them the others fell away and Walking Cat stood face to face with Pike. Pike knew he had picked him because he was bigger than McConnell— hell, he was bigger than almost anyone. Walking Cat had to show his braves that he wasn't afraid of the big white man.

"Untie him," Walking Cat said in English.

One of his braves went behind the tree and cut Pike's bonds. Immediately, Pike felt the blood begin to flow back into his hands.

14

"What about my friend?"

Walking Cat flicked his eyes to McConnell and then looked back at Pike. He had to look up, because he was several inches shorter than Pike.

"He will stay tied."

"Why?"

Walking Cat smiled tightly.

"Because I will fight you one at a time."

"Fight us?" Pike asked. "For what?"

"For Sun Rising."

"Sun Rising?"

"My squaw," Walking Cat said. "The one you and your friend tried to steal."

"We didn't try to steal her, Walking Cat," Pike said. "She wanted to come with us, but —"

"And you were going to take her," Walking Cat said. "That is stealing."

"We *weren't* going to take her," Pike said.

"Your friend was caught with her," Walking Cat said, pointing to McConnell.

"I was, uh, telling her that she couldn't come with us," McConnell said.

Still staring at Pike, Walking Cat said, "When he was found Sun Rising was naked."

Pike closed his eyes, then turned his head and looked at McConnell, who shrugged helplessly.

"All right," Pike said, "we fight. What happens if I win?"

"Then you will go free."

"And my friend?"

"He will fight for his own freedom."

Pike knew he had a chance against Walking Cat, but he wasn't sure that McConnell did. He might have to kill him to protect McConnell. What would the other braves do if that happened?

"When will we fight?" Pike asked.

"Now."

"How?"

15

"With knives."

"A fight to the death?"

Walking Cat nodded and said, "A fight to the death."

"Tell me something, Walking Cat," Pike said.

"What?"

"If I kill you, what will happen to me? And to my friend?"

"That will be up to them," Walking Cat said. "And whoever they choose as their new leader."

Pike shook his head and said, "I'm afraid that's not good enough."

Walking Cat frowned.

"Before I fight, I need a guarantee."

"What kind of . . . guarantee?"

"If I win, we both go free."

Walking Cat's gaze never wavered, but Pike thought he saw something behind the man's eyes.

"Wait," he said, finally, and he and the other braves walked off.

"What are you doing?" McConnell asked.

"I'm getting us out of here alive."

"You're gonna push them into killing us."

"No," Pike said. "These braves have no courage."

"Don't tell them that."

"No, I mean it. That's why they're camped out here and not with the main party."

"They had the courage to leave their chief."

"He was their courage," Pike said. "They didn't realize that, and when they left him they left their courage behind. They thought that Walking Cat could lead them, but I'm about to prove that he can't."

Pike and McConnell watched as Walking Cat talked with four of his braves, then the five Indians walked back to them.

"As you wish," Walking Cat said. "If you defeat me, if you kill me, you and your friend will go free."

Pike felt a surge of satisfaction. He had made Walking Cat change his decision. That would not sit well with the

16

rest of his men. The other four braves did not look happy.

Pike decided to try and push it a bit further.

"Walking Cat, this is not right."

"What is not right?"

"That two men such as us should fight, and that one should kill the other over a squaw."

There was a flash in the brave's eyes and Pike knew immediately that he had made a mistake. He had tried to push the man one step too far.

"She is not *a* squaw," Walking Cat said, "she is *my* squaw, and for trying to steal her from me, I will kill you both."

Pike looked over at McConnell, who simply shrugged. There wasn't much else he could do except watch Pike fight for both their lives.

Ivan Koloff looked down at the people scattered below him and his party.

"They look like . . . Indians," Leonid said.

"Yes," Koloff replied, "all but two."

"White men," Vanya said. "Americans."

At that moment both Colonel Uri Makarov and Charles Severance joined them.

"What's going on?" Severance asked.

"It looks as if two white men—mountain men, by their looks—have been captured by some Indians." Koloff frowned, studying the Indians more closely. "If my research is correct, they are Crow. Mr. Severance?"

Severance looked surprised at the question.

"Mr. Koloff, I'm afraid I know nothing of Indians. They are not, uh, within my purview."

"Crow Indians, then," Koloff said, depending on his own knowledge.

"Look," Vanya said.

They watched with interest while one white man, the larger of the two, seemed to be squaring off against one of the Indians.

"They are about to do battle," Koloff observed.

"Shall we rescue them?" Colonel Makarov asked Koloff. "We have the weapons."

"Indeed," Koloff replied, "but let us wait and see what happens."

"That man could be killed," Severance said.

"Mr. Severance, you're acting as my guide. You have no authority to tell me what I can and cannot do. At this point, I do not wish to risk the safety of my people to save two mountain men."

Severance did not have the backbone to argue with Koloff, so he fell silent as they watched the men below prepare for battle.

Pike took a deep breath, filling his lungs with the icy air of the Rockies, which he loved so much. As a last thought he removed his shirt. The cold air bit into his skin, but he relished that also.

"I'm ready," Pike said to Walking Cat.

Walking Cat was preparing for combat himself.

"Give him a knife," he said to a nearby brave.

"If you don't mind," Pike said, "I'd like to have my own knife."

The brave paused and looked at Walking Cat.

"Give it to him."

The brave turned and took the knife from a second brave, who seemed reluctant to give it up.

With his own knife in hand Pike felt a little better.

But just a little.

"How interesting," Koloff said. "They are going to fight with knives."

"Like gypsies," Leonid remarked.

"We can't just stay here and watch," Severance said warily.

Koloff looked at him, then said, "Perhaps you are right.

Leonid, have the others come forward with their weapons. If the Indians kills the mountain man, we might have to save the other one."

"As you wish."

Satisfied that he had taken some action, Koloff once again directed his attention to the impending battle.

Personally, he thought the mountain man would do very nicely indeed.

They circled each other for the first few moments. Pike was intent on testing Walking Cat's patience. He was certainly in no hurry to die, so he had no intention of rushing in until he had studied the man for a while.

As it turned out, Walking Cat did not have very much patience. He slashed at Pike several times, each time coming closer and closer. Pike moved back just enough to avoid the blade, and timed Walking Cat's movement. When he thought that he had the man figured out, he dropped down off the balls of his feet and waited.

This time when Walking Cat swung and stepped in, Pike moved back just far enough to avoid the swing of the man's arm, then stepped forward quickly before Walking Cat could bring his arm back. He caught the brave's arm around the wrist, turned the knife, and brought his other hand down hard on Walking Cat's elbow, using the handle of his own knife as a club. Walking Cat's arm bent at an unnatural angle, but to the brave's credit he did not scream.

When Pike released his grip, Walking Cat stepped back and reached over with his left hand and plucked the knife from his right before it could fall from his nerveless fingers. Sweat had broken out on Walking Cat's brow, and Pike was sure that it was a result of the shock of having his arm broken.

His right arm hanging uselessly at his side, Walking Cat continued to stalk Pike, holding the knife ready in his left hand.

"Walking Cat," Pike said, "you have only one arm. Let's call this off, and my friend and I will be on our way."

Walking Cat did not respond. His eyes were intent on Pike as he moved forward, the knife held out in front of him. He seemed to have learned his lesson, and was no longer slashing blindly at Pike. Instead, he seemed intent on moving in as close as he could before he made another try.

Pike decided that Walking Cat was probably not a very good knife fighter. Why he had chosen knives over hand-to-hand combat was a mystery only the brave could answer. Maybe Walking Cat was intimidated by Pike's size and did not want to face him without a weapon.

Yeah, maybe that was it . . . intimidation . . .

Abruptly, Pike stood up and tossed his knife aside. It landed at the feet of one of the watching braves.

Walking Cat straightened up and stared at Pike in confusion. The same look was mirrored on the faces of all the observers—including the trussed up McConnell and the very interested Ivan Koloff and company . . .

"Why did he do that?" Leonid wondered aloud.

"Come, Leonid," Koloff said. "Even we use this same tactic with some of the animals that we hunt."

Leonid looked at his master and said, "Intimidation?"

"Of course," Koloff said. "First he renders the Indian's arm useless, now he insults him—or *intimidates* him—by tossing away his knife. He is telling the man, 'I do not need this knife to defeat you.' I am very impressed by this man."

"Come on, Walking Cat," Pike said, waving the brave closer. "Let's get this over with. My friend and I have other things to do."

As Pike had hoped, he had so humiliated Walking Cat

in front of his people that he threw caution to the wind and charged.

Pike sidestepped, sticking his foot out and tripping the brave as he went by. As Walking Cat began to fall Pike moved like a panther and pounced on the man's back, using his weight to drive the man to the ground. As they landed they both grunted with the impact, Walking Cat taking the worst of it. The air seemed to go out of the Indian and he lay motionless on the ground beneath Pike.

Pike got up and cautiously rolled the man over. As he did so he saw that the brave's own knife had buried itself to the hilt in his belly. It took only a second for him to decide that Walking Cat was dead.

Pike stood up, looking down at his vanquished foe, and then looked up at the other braves. They were all watching him, and to a man, the looks on their faces were looks of hatred.

Pike walked over to where McConnell was tied and freed his friend.

"Look at them," Skins McConnell said, rubbing his wrists.

Two braves were leaning over their dead leader, satisfying themselves that he was indeed dead, while the others continued to stare at Pike and McConnell.

"Pike," McConnell said, "I don't think they're going to let us go."

"If they kill us," Pike said, "they will lose all semblance of dignity and honor."

"Look at their faces, Pike," McConnell said, "I don't think they care about that."

Pike studied the faces of the Indians and agreed with McConnell.

They were not going to let them go.

"Marvelous!" Ivan Koloff said. Even from where he stood he could see the knife sticking out from the Indian's belly. "Beautifully done. I'm very impressed with my first

21

mountain man."

"I do not think you should be too impressed," Leonid said. "Look."

Koloff looked and realized that the other Indians were not prepared to let the two mountain men go now that their leader was dead.

"No honor," he said.

"What shall we do?" Leonid asked.

"Do?" Koloff asked. "Why, commence firing, of course."

Leonid turned to the others and shouted, "Fire!"

"Here it comes," McConnell said.

"Well, let's see how many of the sons of bitches we can take with us," Pike said to his friend.

As they braced themselves for the charge they suddenly heard shots. The Crow braves, the ones who had not been cut down by the barrage of lead, turned and ran for cover or for their horses.

Pike and McConnell flattened themselves on the ground, lest they be struck by a stray bullet, and continued to watch.

Some of the Indians actually made it to their horses, but whoever was firing was very good. Before long the ground was strewed with dead Crow braves. Pike figured that at best one or two might have escaped.

Pike and McConnell stood up and began to look for their rescuers.

"There," Pike said at last, pointing to a party riding down from a peak that must have been their vantage point.

"I wonder how long they were watching before they decided to take a hand?" McConnell mused.

"I don't know," Pike said. "Maybe we should ask them."

Chapter Two

After introductions were made and Pike and McConnell had thanked the Russians for their help, the Russian party decided to make camp right there. Koloff ordered his men to clean away the bodies of the Crow, after which they pitched their tents. Pike and McConnell were invited to share their camp and their food.

They sat with Koloff around the fire in front of his tent while dinner was cooked around a communal fire in the center of the camp.

"I was very impressed by your performance, Mr. Pike," Koloff said.

"Just how long were you watching?" Pike asked. He had wanted to ask the question immediately upon meeting them, but thought it would be rude. Now seemed to be the right time.

"Long enough to see you acquit yourself quite well," Koloff answered. "Tell me, why were you and your friend captives of the savages?"

McConnell looked at Pike, who left it to him to answer.

"A difference of opinion," McConnell said finally.

"And that was enough to force a fight to the death?" Koloff asked.

"Very often, in the mountains, a fight like that is the only way to settle something," McConnell replied. "We have very little in the way of law up here. What we have we pretty much make ourselves."

"How fascinating."

Just then a woman came out of Koloff's tent. They had seen her previously, but had not had the pleasure of being introduced.

"Ah, gentlemen," Koloff said, rising. Pike and McConnell stood up as well. "Allow me to introduce Vanya Ivoroff."

Pike and McConnell both allowed as how they were pleased to meet her. In fact, it was a pleasure just to look at her. She was tall, dark-haired, pale-skinned, with a full figure and very long legs.

Vanya sat down on a small wooden stool, and Leonid brought over plates of food for the hungry guests.

"Buffalo meat," Pike said.

"Yes," Koloff said, "we were lucky enough to encounter a small herd. They smelled us, however, and I only had time for one shot."

"Seems like you made the shot count," Pike said, looking at Koloff's Russian-made rifle. "Are you a good shot?"

Before Koloff could answer Vanya said proudly, "Ivan is the finest shot in all of Russia."

"Is that a fact?" Pike said.

"Yes," she retorted, lifting her chin. "In fact, I would say he is the finest shot in the world."

"That's quite a claim," Pike said. He was willing to let the matter drop, but McConnell was not.

"I gotta tell you, miss," McConnell said, "Pike here is the best shot I ever seen."

"Really?" Koloff said with genuine interest. "Do you hunt, Mr. Pike?"

Pike laughed for a moment, then said, "There's not much else for us to do up here but hunt, Mr. Koloff."

"Please, please," Koloff said, "we are new friends, no? Call me Ivan."

"Well, Ivan," McConnell said, "I'd be willing to put

Pike here up against you in a shooting contest."

"Skins . . ." Pike said, warning in his voice.

"You would not be willing to compete against me in such a contest?" Koloff asked Pike.

"It's not that," Pike replied. "As you just said, we're new friends."

"Then we can have a friendly competition, no?" Koloff asked.

Sensing that he was not going to be allowed to back down, Pike said, "Sure. Why not?"

Pike and McConnell had been able to recover their guns after their rescue, but their horses had run off with the rest of their supplies.

"In the morning I will have my men search for your horses," Koloff said. "I would not want to leave you here on foot."

"We appreciate that," Pike said.

"While we wait for them to return we can have our friendly little competition, yes?"

"Sure," Pike said, glaring at McConnell. "Why not?"

Koloff had made his men double up so that Pike and McConnell could use one of the tents.

"What the hell was that all about?" Pike asked.

"What?"

"Challenging Ivan to a shooting contest," Pike said. "What was the big idea?"

"Well, we couldn't just let him go on saying he was the best shot in the world, could we?"

"Why not?" Pike asked. "And *he* didn't say it, she did."

"You want her to think we can't shoot?"

"What do you mean, *we?*" Pike said. "You challenged him on *my* behalf!"

"Well, you're a better shot than I am."

"Skins," Pike said, "these people saved our bacon for us. We've got no business challenging them."

"He likes the idea."

"How much is he going to like it if I beat him?"

"If?" McConnell said. "You mean when, don't you?"

"If, when, what's the difference?" Pike said. "It's just a way to pass the time while they look for our horses. That's how I look at it."

"Well, I look at it like our pride is at stake," McConnell said.

"*Our* pride?"

"Sure," McConnell said, "tomorrow you'll be shooting against Ivan for the pride of all mountain men—hell, all Americans."

"That's crazy," Pike said.

"You think so? Wait until we get to the next settlement and you'll see what everyone thinks when we tell them you won."

"Or lost."

"Don't think that way."

"Look," Pike said, "I'm going out for a walk before I turn in."

"I'll clean your rifle for you."

Pike was going to protest, but instead he just shrugged and said, "Fine."

Pike went walking through the camp, nodding at two of Koloff's men. He didn't know whether or not they could speak English, having heard only Koloff, Vanya, and Leonid speak it. He wondered about Severance. The man said very little, even when they were introduced, and he seemed to defer to Koloff in all things. Pike wondered just what Severance was supposed to be doing.

By the time he reached the edge of the camp he didn't expect to encounter anyone, so when he heard footfalls he stopped abruptly, his hand touching his Kentucky pistol tucked into his belt.

"Do not shoot," a female voice said. It was Vanya, coming out of the shadows toward him.

"What are you doing out here?" he asked.

"I suspect the same thing you are doing," she said. "Walking."

"You shouldn't be out here alone."

"I am not," Vanya said. "You are here."

As if to make her point she moved closer to Pike.

"I was very impressed with you today," she continued. "I do not think I had the opportunity to tell you."

"Thank you."

"I was excited, also."

"Excited?"

"Yes," she said, "excited—sexually excited."

Pike thought he saw where this was leading, only this time it would be the Russians tying them to a tree instead of the Indians.

"You're Ivan's woman, aren't you?"

"Yes," she said, "but that does not mean that another man cannot excite me."

"I don't mind exciting you," Pike said, "just don't ask me to go any further."

"I will not ask," Vanya said, smiling, and then added, "Not now, that is."

"Vanya—"

"Good night, Pike," she said. "I will see you in the morning."

"Good night."

She started to walk away, then turned back. Her face was flushed from the cold, her usually pale cheeks reddened. Vapor came from her mouth in quick, short bursts.

"I wish you luck tomorrow," she said. "Ivan is a fine shot, as I said."

"I'll do my best," Pike said. "If I win, I win."

"And if you lose?"

Pike shrugged. "Then I lose."

She frowned and said, "Ivan does not feel that way. He wants to win at all costs."

"Will I make an enemy if I defeat him?"

She hesitated a moment before answering.

"Don't even think about letting him win," she said finally. "He will know if you are not trying your very best to beat him."

"How?"

"He always gives his best, and he recognizes it in others."

"I always try my best."

"Then what will happen will happen," she said. "You should not worry about the consequences."

She turned and this time walked away.

Koloff was lying on a bed of pillows when Vanya entered the tent.

"Where did you go?" he asked.

"Just for a walk."

"What did you see?"

"Nothing," she said, removing her coat. "The sky, the stars . . . oh, and I saw Mr. Pike."

"Really?" he asked, watching her as she removed her clothes. "What did you talk about?"

Naked, she walked to where he lay, her breasts swaying.

"We talked about you."

"About me?" Koloff said, laughing. "The mountain man and the beautiful woman, and you spoke of me?"

She ran her hands over his hairy chest and whispered, "What else would I talk about?"

He laughed softly, closing his powerful arms around her.

"Ivan—" she said, feeling his arms tighten around her.

"I saw the way you were watching him this afternoon, when he was fighting," Koloff said.

"You are holding me tightly—" Her breath was coming with difficulty.

"My love," Koloff said, nuzzling her neck while continuing to hold her, "you must remember who brought you to this country."

"I remember—"

"And you must remember who will leave you here if you displease me."

"I will not—"

"I know you will not," he said, relaxing his hold on her. His arms were still around her, but she was able to breathe easily now.

He stroked her face, kissed her cheek, and cupped her breast. Then he pushed her down until her face was level with his crotch . . .

Colonel Uri Makarov sat in his tent cleaning his weapon. He had served Ivan Koloff for many years and had learned to read the man's moods, the man's expressions.

Koloff was tiring of hunting animals. The bear would be the last one, and then Koloff would want to hunt something new, something different . . .

Makarov knew how impressed Koloff was with Pike, and if the man managed to beat him in the shooting competition tomorrow he would be even more impressed.

If he was defeated, however, Koloff would not be a happy man . . . and Makarov had seen many times the kind of man Koloff was when he was unhappy . . .

Charles Severance didn't know what he was doing here. He had told his superiors that he was not the man for this job, but they had assured him that all he would have to do was to ride along with the Russians and keep them happy.

Lately he had been finding it harder to talk with Koloff, harder to keep him happy. Severance was fed up with the mountain life, the animals, the dust, the sleeping on the ground. He'd had enough of watching Vanya Ivoroff every day, of listening to the grunting and groaning of her and Koloff's rutting every night . . . Charles Severance wanted to go home . . .

"Thanks a lot," Pike said as he reentered the tent.

"For what?" McConnell asked.

"For putting me in a position to make a new enemy."

"Koloff?"

Pike nodded and told him about his conversation with Vanya.

"If he's that competitive, he should appreciate you more for beating him."

"Skins, you and I have both known competitive people. They enjoy the competition as long as they win."

McConnell put Pike's newly cleaned rifle down and rubbed his jaw.

"You think I made a mistake?"

Pike opened his mouth to answer, then thought better of it. When he finally spoke he said something other than what he'd first intended.

"I think we should just take Vanya's advice, at this point."

"What advice?"

"I'll do the best I can and not worry about the consequences."

Chapter Three

Pike was up early the next morning. He wished they were closer to a lake so he could take a morning swim. As long as the sun was out, he enjoyed dunking himself in the water even on the coldest of mornings.

As he stepped out of the tent he saw that he was not the first to rise. Leonid was already setting the coffee pot onto the fire.

"Good morning, Leonid," Pike said.

The man looked up at him, his face expressionless, and said, "Good morning."

"You speak English very well."

"Thank you."

"You also make good coffee."

The compliment seemed to please the man.

"That I learn from my mother."

"She made good coffee, eh?"

"She was wonderful cook," Leonid said. Pike realized for the first time that Leonid was probably not yet thirty years old. "When I was little boy, the smells of her cooking would bring me running home, even if I was playing with my friends."

"It sounds wonderful."

"Your mother was good cook?"

Pike rubbed at the ground with his right foot and said,

"I never knew my mother. She died giving birth to me."

"That is too bad," Leonid said sympathetically. "You were raised by your father?"

"Yes," Pike said, and then added, "when he was around he raised me."

When the coffee was ready Leonid poured two cups. Pike expected him to take both cups to Koloff's tent, one for Koloff and one for Vanya. Instead, Leonid surprised him by handing him one of the cups.

"Do not tell him I gave you the first cup, eh?" Leonid said in a conspiratorial whisper.

"I'll never tell."

As Leonid brought Koloff his morning cup of coffee Pike walked around the camp with his. The morning was a clear one, and Pike suddenly wondered if the one or two Crow braves who escaped might not come back with others.

Leonid returned to the fire and said to Pike, "He asked me to tell you that his men would be going out shortly to find your horses."

"I think we should move away from here quickly," Pike said. "The crow couild return at any time."

"I will wake the others," Leonid said, "so that the search may start."

"All right."

Pike finished his coffee, then poured another cup and took it into the tent.

"Wake up," he said, holding the coffee out to McConnell.

McConnell sat up, rubbing his eyes and stretching his back, then took the coffee.

"Thanks. What's going on?"

"They're getting ready to start the search."

"What about the contest?"

"Maybe he forgot about it."

"You believe that?"

"No," Pike said, "but shooting might bring the Crow back."

"How many you figure got away?"

"One, maybe two," Pike said, "or three, counting Sun Rising."

"Yeah, what *did* happen to her?" McConnell said. "I didn't see where she went when the shooting started."

"I didn't, either."

"You think they'll come back?"

"Not really," Pike said. "First they'll have to get brave enough to go back to the tribe and explain themselves to their chief. That alone should give us plenty of time to leave—but there are other Indians, and the shooting could attract any of them."

"Well," McConnell said, pushing himself up, "maybe you can convince him of that."

Outside they heard movement, and while McConnell dressed, Pike went out to see what was going on. He saw three of Koloff's men saddling their horses. At that moment Koloff himself appeared outside his tent. The man paused, took a deep breath, and then approached his men and spoke to them briefly. That done he spotted Pike and walked over to join him.

"Did you sleep well, Pike?"

"Yes, thank you."

"Are you ready for our little competition?" Koloff asked, rubbing his hands together. "Nothing makes my blood race like competition, whether it is between man and beast or man and man."

"Well, I wanted to talk to you about that."

"You do not want to go through with it?"

"That's not it," Pike said, although he wondered why he was saying that. He should have just told Koloff that was right, he *didn't* want to go through with it, but there was that matter of pride that McConnell had spoken about. Pike didn't want Koloff to think that he was afraid to shoot against him.

"I think that we should postpone it until we reach a settlement. After all, there are other Indians in these mountains beside the Crow."

33

"Postpone it?" Koloff asked. He did not seem particularly pleased by the suggestion. "Mr. Pike, isn't it true that living here you run the constant risk of trouble with Indians?"

"Yes."

"And yet you do not—how do you Americans say it—run scared all the time?"

"Of course not," Pike said. "Who could live that way?"

Koloff smiled and said, "Exactly. I will get my rifle, and you get yours. Both Leonid and your friend McConnell can act as judges. Agreed?"

Pike knew he was going to have to go through with it, so he said, "All right, agreed."

"Excellent!"

Koloff went to his tent to fetch his rifle, and Pike turned to find McConnell stepping out of their tent with his rifle.

"I'm sorry I got you into this thing, Pike," McConnell said.

"Forget it," Pike said, taking the rifle. "Let's get this over with and get out of here. If Koloff's men don't find our horses we'll just walk away from here. We've done that before."

"You're gonna outshoot him, ain't you?"

"If I don't I'll want to know the reason why," Pike replied.

"Ooh . . ." McConnell whispered. Pike turned and saw what had so impressed his friend. Vanya Ivoroff had come out of the tent, her hands up over her head. She was holding her hair up so that the cold breeze could strike the back of her neck.

She walked across to where Pike and McConnell were standing, still holding her hair over her head and smiling at them.

"It feels like home here in your mountains," she greeted Pike. "I like them."

"So do we," Pike said.

"Ivan is seeing to his rifle. He wanted me to ask you to

pick out your targets."

Pike looked around and saw a tree with branches of many sizes. They could start with the largest ones and work their way down to the smallest . . . or they could simply start with the smallest.

"I need some coffee," Vanya said, but made no move to get it herself.

"I'll get it for you," McConnell volunteered, and hurried past her.

"Thank you," she called after him. She turned back to Pike and said, "He's very thoughtful, your friend."

"Yeah," Pike replied, thinking that's how they had gotten into the mess with the Crow in the first place. He knew little about Russians, much less than he did about Crow, and wondered what kind of mess they were getting into now.

Koloff came out of his tent with his rifle and shouted, "Shall we get started?"

"Sure," Pike said. "Why not?"

They had completely forgotten about Charles Severance, the only other person still in camp besides Colonel Markarov. As Koloff's personal bodyguard, Makarov never left his master's side. Now Severance and Makarov took up positions on opposite sides of the camp to watch the contest.

"That tree," McConnell said, pointing. "Let's forget about the big branches. Shoot off the smallest branch you can see."

"All right," Koloff said. "As a guest in your country, I suggest that I should go first."

Pike smiled. "Of course."

Koloff shouldered his rifle, sighted down the barrel, and fired. A branch thinner than a man's little finger disappeared.

"Good shot."

"I am afraid that since I shot off the smallest branch

35

you will not be able to match it."

Pike stared at the tree for a few moments, then said, "We'll see," and shouldered his rifle.

Below the branch that Koloff had shot off there was a sprout so small that it could not even be called a branch. It was all green, with no brown, but it was there. Koloff had either not seen it or had discounted it.

Pike fired and the twig disappeared.

McConnell and Leonid both walked to the tree, discussed the shots, and then McConnell called out, "Pike wins."

Severance flinched, wishing that Pike had had the good sense to let Koloff win.

Leonid looked away as Koloff glared at him.

"Shooting at branches is silly," Koloff announced. "Moving targets are more of a challenge. Leonid! Toss a cup in the air."

Leonid nodded. He walked to the fire and picked up a tin cup.

"Ready?" he asked.

"Ready," Koloff said, and shouldered his rifle.

Leonid reared back and threw the cup as high and as hard as he could. Koloff sighted down the barrel, waited for the cup to reach its zenith, and then fired. There was a sharp *ping* as the bullet found its mark.

"Nice shot," Pike said again.

"Thank you," Koloff said, obviously pleased with the shot himself.

"Skins."

"I got it," McConnell said.

He picked up the same cup and walked back to the fire with it.

"Ready?"

"Ready."

McConnell reared back and threw the cup as hard as he could. It might have gone higher than when Leonid threw it, but Pike didn't give it a chance. He fired *before* the cup reached its zenith, striking the cup and jarring it from its

36

trajectory.

McConnell and Leonid walked to where the cup had fallen. Since Pike's shot had struck the cup before it reached its zenith, McConnell called out, "Pike wins." Charles Severance flinched again.

Leonid did not argue.

Koloff turned and looked at Pike, who was already reloading his weapon.

"You are truly a fine marksman, Pike."

"So are you."

"I do not think anything can be served by continuing this," Leonid said. "The true test of a marksman—and a hunter—comes in the face of game."

"Of course."

"I am hunting your brown bear," Koloff said. "I understand it is one of the largest bears in the world."

"I've known grizzlies that measured over nine feet and weighed over a thousand pounds."

"Indeed," Koloff said, raising his eyebrows. "That sounds like even more than I had hoped for. I wonder, Pike, if we could not strike a small bargain."

"What did you have in mind?"

"Guide me," Koloff said. "Take me to where I can find this grizzly of such extraordinary size."

"I don't think so, Ivan," Pike said. "McConnell and I have to get to the nearest settlement and reoutfit ourselves."

"I will pay you well," Koloff said, "both of you. Certainly more than enough to outfit you royally."

"I don't think—"

"Think about it," Koloff said. "Wait until the last minute to give me your decision."

"All right," Pike said, "I'll think about it."

"Good," Koloff said, and walked back to his tent. Vanya followed, but glanced back at Pike before following him inside.

Severance came walking over to Pike very quickly and said peevishly, "You could have let him win, you know."

"He wanted to win, Mr. Severance," Pike said, "but he wouldn't have wanted me to let him win."

"Well, anyway, you can agree to guide him."

"I don't want to guide him."

From between clenched teeth he said, "The United States government wants you to guide him."

"Sorry," Pike said, "I have other plans."

"Change—"

"Sorry," Pike said again, and turned and walked away from Severance, leaving him sputtering.

Inside their tent McConnell said, "It could mean a lot of money to us to guide him, Pike."

"What were we on our way to do before we got caught up with those Crow?"

McConnell frowned and said, "Damned if I can remember."

"We were . . ." Pike started to speak, then stopped as he realized that they had really been doing nothing. They had been drifting, unsure of what they wanted to do with their time.

"See?" McConnell said. "What have we got to lose? And we have a lot to gain. Let's charge him a lot."

"And if we can't find him a bear?"

"We'll find him a bear, Pike," McConnell said, "we know where to look."

"What if we don't find one big enough to satisfy him?"

"That's his problem. We'll just have to make arrangements with him for the money to be paid no matter what size the bear is," McConnell said. "Dicker with him, Pike, you're good at that."

"I can dicker for fur prices," Pike said, lamenting to himself that those days were probably gone forever. These days you took the prices the fur companies gave you and were happy to be able to sell them at all.

"How different can this be?" McConnell asked. "You name a price, he names a price, and you meet somewhere in the middle."

Pike was about to say something when they heard the sound of horses outside.

"Sounds like they found our horses," Pike said.

They went outside to look. Sure enough, Koloff's men had found both of their horses, with their saddles intact.

The Russians had also found something else, something that Pike and McConnell were not all that happy to see again.

"Oh, Jesus," McConnell said.

"Oh, this is just great," Pike said.

Sitting astride an Indian pony in the center of camp was the cause of all their trouble the previous day.

The Russians had brought the Crow squaw, Sun Rising, back to camp with them.

Chapter Four

Koloff also came out of his tent when he heard the horses, joining Pike and McConnell in the center of the camp.

"This is not a good idea, Ivan," Pike said, as McConnell checked their horses.

"What is not a good idea?" Koloff asked.

"Bringing the Indian woman into camp," Pike said. "She's the reason we were trussed up the way we were when you happened along."

Koloff examined Sun Rising, who was still sitting astride her pony. She showed no inclination to leave the camp. She was sitting on her horse proudly, her chin held high.

"She is lovely," Koloff said.

"Yes, she is—"

"Was her man among the Indians we killed?"

"Yes."

"Then I do not see the problem."

"She's a Crow squaw," Pike said.

"The Crow do not want me," Sun Rising said in surprisingly good English.

All eyes turned to her, including those of Vanya, who

had just stepped from the tent she shared with Koloff.

"What do you mean?" Koloff asked.

"Walking Cat is dead," she said. "The two braves who escaped told the others it was my doing. They turned me out. I have no people."

"Would you like to stay with us?" Koloff asked.

Sun Rising looked at Pike and said, "I would like to stay with him."

Koloff looked at Pike with interest.

"Why him?"

"He is Pike."

"What does that mean?"

"His name is legend," she announced. "He is the man whose head touches the sky."

Koloff, looking amused, asked Pike, "Is that true? Are you a legend, Pike?"

"Legends are dead," Pike said. "Do I look dead to you, Ivan?"

"You are wrong, my friend," Koloff said. "Legends are very much alive, and their legend continues to grow with the man. I think perhaps she is right."

Koloff turned to Leonid and said, "Give the woman some food and then get ready to break camp."

Leonid nodded and helped Sun Rising down from her pony.

"We must talk," Koloff said to Pike. "Will you come to my tent?"

Pike looked at McConnell, who nodded.

"The horses are in good shape," he said. "I'll check our gear."

"All right," Pike said, and then turned to Koloff. "I'll listen to what you have to say, Ivan," he replied.

"Come then," Koloff said, and led the way to his tent.

On his way through camp Pike passed Severance, who gave Pike what was meant to be a meaningful look. To Pike, however, he looked like a man who hadn't been able to heed the call of nature for three days.

Vanya, standing just outside the tent, was still studying

41

Sun Rising with interest.

"See to the Indian woman," Koloff said to her, and entered the tent.

Vanya gave Pike a bold look as he followed Koloff into the tent.

Inside, Koloff was holding a bottle of clear liquid.

"Russian vodka, the finest drink in the world. Will you have one?"

"Sure."

Koloff picked up two tin cups, poured two fingers of vodka into each, and handed one to Pike. Pike sniffed it and found it had virtually no odor. He tasted it and decided it was not bad at all.

"How is it?" Koloff asked.

"It's fine," Pike said, "just fine."

"Pike," Koloff continued, "I am even more determined now to hire you as my guide—you and your friend."

"Why?" Pike asked. "Because you think I'm a legend?"

"I think you are the man to show me what I wish to see," Koloff said. "I doubt that I will find one better."

Pike didn't comment.

"I will pay you well," Koloff said, "very well, indeed."

Pike frowned and finished his vodka. He did not have the right to agree or refuse until he spoke with McConnell about it.

"I'll talk to Skins," he said, putting the tin cup down. "I'll let you know by the time we break camp."

"Excellent."

"And I suggest we break camp soon," Pike added.

"I will see to it," Koloff replied. "What about the Indian woman?"

Pike shrugged. "Let's decide what we're going to do before we decide what to do with her."

"Agreed."

Pike left the tent and walked across the camp to where McConnell was standing with the horses.

"Well?" McConnell asked.

"Gear all here?"

"Most of it," McConnell said. "No food, though. Looks like the Crow ate that pretty quick. What happened with Koloff?"

"Well, he's offering us a lot of money."

"You mean he's offering *you* a lot of money."

"It looked like he took that 'legend' remark to heart."

"I guess."

"I suspect that raised his price a little."

"I suspect."

"Well, what do you think?"

"I think we could probably use the money," Pike said.

"I believe you're right."

Pike knew that McConnell wanted to take the job, at least for a while.

"Well then," Pike said, "I might as well dicker us a price."

"It don't seem like you'll have much dickering to do, as bad as he wants you."

"I just got one thing to say about this."

"What?"

"I ain't doing no play acting to live up to no legend," Pike said, with conviction. "I ain't doing nothing I don't ordinarily do."

"*I* wouldn't ask you to," McConnell said. "What are we going to do about her?"

Pike turned to see both Vanya and Sun Rising looking their way.

"Which one you talking about?"

McConnell took a moment to consider the question and then said, "I guess both of them. They both got eyes for you."

"Don't start that," Pike said. "We had enough trouble with Sun Rising as it is. I don't need trouble from two women."

"Sun Rising hasn't got a man to worry about now," McConnell said. "Her people have turned her out. My guess is you could do just about anything you wanted with her."

"Well, Vanya does have a man, and he's a proud one,"

43

Pike said. "Maybe too proud."

"What's that mean?"

"It means I don't think Ivan Koloff and I will ever really be friends."

By the break of camp Pike had "dickered" his price with Koloff, and a high price it was—so high and so easily agreed to that Pike thought he probably could have gotten even more.

Once it was announced that he would guide Koloff and his party, Pike explained that they would first have to stop at Clark's Fork, a nearby settlement, to properly outfit themselves. The next problem was what to do with Sun Rising.

"I think we should take her with us," Koloff said. "I cannot think of leaving her out here alone."

"She wouldn't be alone for long," Pike countered. "Lots of men are looking for a good squaw."

"She should be able to find a man at the settlement with no problem . . . wouldn't you think?"

Weary of the issue, Pike finally relented, and it was agreed that she would travel to the settlement with them. Pike had an uncomfortable feeling about the whole thing, but he and McConnell would have to work awfully hard and long to make even a fraction of what Ivan Koloff was paying them.

Pike was impressed with the horsemanship everyone in Koloff's party showed—even Vanya. Of course, the best rider of them all was Sun Rising, who sat bareback on her horse with supreme confidence.

Pike and McConnell rode the point, with Koloff and Leonid right behind. Further back rode Severance and Makarov, then Vanya and Sun Rising, followed by the other men in Koloff's party.

During the entire two-day trip to Clark's Fork, Pike and

44

McConnell never spoke to Sun Rising, not even when they camped. They both remembered what happened the last time one of them showed interest in her.

To Pike's surprise, it was Vanya who paid Sun Rising the most attention. During each meal the two women sat off to themselves, talking animatedly. It was clear that the Crow and the Russian were becoming good friends.

Physically, they were very much alike. Both were dark-haired, tall, full-bodied, and close to thirty—Sun Rising perhaps a little younger, Vanya a little older. The one striking difference between the two women, of course, was that Sun Rising's skin was dark while Vanya's was very pale.

Another thing they both seemed to have in common was an interest in Pike. He often caught one or both of them staring at him, and at such times he made a point of looking the other way.

The trading post at Clark's Fork had started out small but had grown by leaps and bounds. Ted Clark had built himself a little business, and the settlement of Clark's Fork had grown up around him, expanding even during the few months since Pike and McConnell had last been there. It was now two blocks long, with wooden structures and tents on either side of the main "street." The last time they had been there Pike had found out that Ted Clark had been named honorary mayor, and he had no reason to think that had changed.

At the end of the first block stood a primitive livery assembled out of wood and a tent. The wooden structure housed the horses; the tent served as the liveryman's home and office. The last time they were there it had been at the very end of the settlement. It now stood smack in the center of it, with another "block" going on beyond it.

"We'll put our animals up here," Pike said. He turned and looked at Koloff. "There is no hotel, but you can pitch your tents at the end of the street."

"Very well," Koloff said.

He dismounted and gave his men instructions. Some of them were to see to the horses, others to the erecting of the tents.

Pike dismounted and said to Koloff, "Skins and I have to say hello to some friends. We also have to outfit ourselves. You'll probably have to replenish your supplies too."

Koloff took out a wad of money and handed the whole thing to Pike.

"I will trust you to take care of that."

Pike looked at the money in his hand and said, "This is too much."

"Use what you must and return the rest," Koloff said.

"You trust me with this much money?"

"Of course," Koloff said. "Why would I not?"

Pike looked at McConnell and tucked the money away in a pocket.

"We'll meet you after a little while," Pike said to Koloff.

"What about Sun Rising?" McConnell asked.

Vanya answered that question.

"She will share a tent with me."

Koloff looked at Vanya, then grinned and said to Leonid, "I guess that means you and I will be sharing a tent, old friend."

"As you wish," Leonid replied with a shrug.

Pike turned to go. "We'll see you in a while," he called.

When they entered the trading post, Pike and Skins saw Ted Clark behind his makeshift bar. He still clung to this rude counter, even though he could now afford to have a real bar shipped in if he wanted. To Clark, however, the original bar was a reminder of how his business had started, a symbol of how it had grown.

Off to the right, behind another counter, was Clark's Crow wife, the beautiful Sky Woman.

Ted Clark was a strapping man. He was over six feet and weighed in excess of two hundred pounds. From the looks of his belly, he now weighed *well* over two hundred pounds. The full beard was also new. Though not quite as full as Pike's, it was still full enough to change the look of him, making him appear ten years older in the bargain.

"Ted, you old . . . sonofagun," Pike said. He caught himself, changing what he had originally intended to say in deference to Sky Woman's presence.

"Pike! Skins!" Ted Clark roared happily. Sky Woman looked up from what she was doing and smiled. It was not so much that she was glad to see Pike and McConnell, mostly she was smiling at the pleasure that showed on her husband's face.

"Well, look at you," Pike said. He approached the bar, leaned over it, and patted Clark's burgeoning belly. "Sky Woman must be stuffing you good and proper."

Clark's belly dwarfed his barrel chest, but when he stuck out his hand it was as big as a ham, just like always—and still hard as a rock.

"It's good to see you boys," Clark said, shaking first Pike's hand and then McConnell's. "You ain't been around in some time, now."

"Well, we're around now," McConnell said, "and we're thirsty."

"Two cold beers, comin' right up," Clark said.

Pike turned and said, "Hello, Sky Woman."

She nodded to them but didn't speak. She rarely spoke, and when she did it was to Clark. She was as beautiful as ever, dark hair and dark skin, like Sun Rising, though not so large. In fact, Sky Woman was almost petite, and seemed even more so whenever she was standing next to her husband.

"Grab a table, boys, and I'll have Sky Woman bring you some stew."

There were four tables in the trading post, made from barrels and two-by-fours.

"Can't turn that down," McConnell said, looking at Pike.

"Why would you want to?" Clark asked.

"We didn't come here alone," Pike said.

"Oh? Who'd you bring with you?"

"Nobody you know," Pike said "but sit with us and we'll explain."

"All right, then," Clark said, *"three* beers, comin' right up."

Chapter Five

Clark listened to Pike's tale, from the fight with the Crow to the encounter with the Russians. While he told his story, he was careful to lower his voice and to stop altogether whenever Sky Woman came within earshot. He was after all, talking about her people.

When Pike was finished Clark said, "Sounds to me like you're a lot better off with these Russians than you were with the Crow."

"That's an understatement," McConnell said. "The Crow were going to kill us and the Russians are going to pay us."

"Where are Russians from, anyway?" Clark asked, frowning.

"From Russia," Pike said.

"Where's that?"

"Damned if I know," Pike admitted, "but I know it ain't in this country."

"Ted," Pike said, rising from the table, "I'll send those Russians over here for some of Sky Woman's stew, and you can get to meet them."

"Well, that'd be fine," Clark said, "but I'm still gonna charge them for the food and drink, even if they are with you."

"If I was you," Pike said, "I'd charge them even more

than usual. Believe me, they can afford it."

"Glad to hear it."

"Speaking of which," Pike said, "Skins is going to give you a list of supplies that we'll need."

"I am?" Skins asked, looking up from his stew. He was still swabbing up gravy with some of Sky Woman's fresh biscuits.

"You are," Pike said. He took out the money Koloff had given him and handed it to McConnell.

"You trust me with this much money?" McConnell asked.

"Just like Koloff trusts me," Pike said.

"And where are you off to?"

"Same place you are when you're finished."

Both McConnell and Clark knew where that was. They exchanged a smile . . .

"You go ahead," McConnell said. "I'll make sure Koloff and the others get to sample Sky Woman's stew."

Ted Clark quickly wiped the smile from his face when his wife entered the room.

As Pike approached the whore's tent he reminded himself that he should be concerned with other things, but the truth was that for the past few days he had been traveling with two beautiful women, both of whom seemed to have eyes for him, and he would have had to be made out of stone not to need a woman at this time. It was a need he wanted to take care of as soon as possible. He planned to move out in the morning, and it looked as if both Vanya and Sun Rising would be coming along on the bear hunt.

As he entered the tent he tried to remember the name of the woman he wanted. He had never had her before, but he remembered the blonde very well from previous visits. How could he forget?

He waited inside, and eventually he was approached by a wide-hipped, dark-haired woman in her mid forties. She was the madam.

"Can I help you, sir?"

"Uh, yes, I would like to, uh, see . . . I'm trying to remember her name."

"Maybe you can describe her?"

"Sure, she's blonde, pale, slender, but with nice, uh—" He was holding his hands out in front of his chest when she rescued him.

"You want Colette."

"Colette! That's her, Colette. Is she available?"

"She's very popular," the madam said. "I'll check. Wait here, please."

While he waited he saw two men escorted out by a couple of partially clad women. Both women looked him up and down with obvious approval, but made no move to entice him.

"Mister?" the madam called.

He looked away from the two women and saw her beckoning to him.

"This way, please."

He followed her, and she led him to a small cubicle fashioned from hanging blankets.

"In there," she said. "Enjoy yourself."

I intend to, he thought, and pushed aside the entry blanket and stepped inside.

"I remember you," Colette said.

He remembered her, too, although the last time he had seen her she'd been totally naked. Now she was wearing a flimsy nightgown, and he could see that she had put on a little weight. Her breasts seemed larger and her hips a little rounder, although her arms and legs were slender. Her blonde hair fell past her breasts, lying on them like a golden veil.

"If I remember correctly," she said, "you had someone else in mind the last time you were here."

"That's right."

"She's not here anymore."

"I know."

"And you asked for me?"

51

"I did."

She moved closer to him. She was about five-seven, but even so she was dwarfed by the size of him—and impressed.

"God," she said, smiling, "you're even bigger than I remember."

"Well," he said, "now that we both remember—"

"Wait," she said, "wait, wait . . . there was something else. Oh, yes, now I remember . . ."

She stepped back and very deftly dropped the nightgown to the ground, leaving herself totally naked. Her nipples were pink and had already begun to pucker.

"Now," she said, moving closer, "this is the way we met last time."

"Yes," he said, "yes, it is."

He remembered from that brief meeting how his hands had itched as she pressed herself to him, and as she snaked toward him now he reached behind her and cupped her buttocks. She lifted her chin and he kissed her, gently at first but then with more urgency as his body began to react to the pressure of hers.

"Let me help you," she said hoarsely, and began to remove his clothes.

"Damn . . ." he said.

"What?"

"I must smell like a mule," he confessed as he slid his legs from his pants.

Now he was totally naked and she was on her knees in front of him. She pressed her face to his belly, wetting him with her tongue, and said, "You smell fine . . . you smell like a man . . ."

She continued to wet him, lapping his navel, moving her mouth and tongue lower until she was faced with his rigid cock.

"Jesus," she said, and licked the spongy head. She grasped him with both hands and allowed him to slide into her mouth, wetting him good.

"Aaah . . ." he groaned, grasping her head lightly.

"Come on, big man," she coaxed, rising from her knees. She took hold of his cock and led him to her bed. The madam must have been doing a good business, because Colette actually had a real bed with a decent mattress.

She slid onto the bed and pulled Pike onto it with her. Then and only then did she release her hold on him as she pushed him down and quickly mounted. She was wet and ready and he slid right into her. She sat astride him, her hands pressed down against his chest, and began to swivel back and forth.

It was all Pike could do to keep from exploding right then and there, but he managed to hold back. He watched her facial expressions with fascination as she started to rock her hips. He'd known a lot of whores, and this one wasn't as cool under fire as most.

She was just plain enjoying herself. And so was he . . .

The Russian party, including Sun Rising and Charlie Severance, took up all four of Ted Clark's makeshift tables. McConnell was at the counter with Ted Clark, having his order filled and paying for it with Koloff's money. Sky Woman was making sure they all had enough to eat. No words had passed between her and Sun Rising . . . yet.

"Excuse me," Koloff said as Sky Woman walked past him. She stopped. "This food is excellent, the best that I have had since coming to your country."

She nodded to him and said, "Thank you."

Sitting with Koloff was Leonid. At the next table sat Sun Rising and Vanya.

Koloff leaned over and asked Sun Rising, "Is she also a Crow woman?"

Sun Rising nodded.

"Can you cook as well as she can?"

"Perhaps."

"Would you like to come with us and cook for us?"

She looked around the room, then asked, "Will Pike be

going?"

"Oh, yes," Koloff said, "Mr. Pike is to be our guide—he and Mr. McConnell."

"Then I will come," she said, "and I will cook."

"Excellent," Koloff said, smiling, "excellent."

Vanya studied him for a moment and decided that he wanted Sun Rising to come along for reasons other than just her cooking.

That was all right with her, because that would leave her free to pursue Pike.

Ted Clark asked McConnell, "Are both those women going to be along on this hunt?"

"Yep."

Clark looked at the women again and then remarked, "That looks like trouble to me."

McConnell took a moment to look over his shoulder at the two women, then looked at Clark and said, "Yep."

"So what got you so hot and bothered that you had to come here looking for me?" Colette asked later.

"What do you mean?"

They were lying side by side in her bed and he was in no hurry to leave.

"I mean you really needed this, even more than a man who's simply come in off the trail after a few weeks."

"You can tell that?"

She smiled and folded her arms beneath her breasts, causing them to rise and swell.

"I've been doing this for a few years, and yes, you get so you can tell the desperate ones."

"And I was desperate?"

"Like a man who's been bothered by a woman who he can't touch."

Pike hesitated a moment and then said, "Or won't."

"Whatever," she said, turning toward him. Her bare

breast pressed up against his arm, and he reached over and stroked it.

"You're not like any whore I ever knew," he said. "You like this, don't you?"

"Not always," she said. "It depends on the man. Take you, for instance. Ever since I first saw you I've been thinking about you, hoping that you would come back."

"I'm flattered."

"Well, so am I," she said. She slid her warm thigh over his and said, "Now that we're both flattered, are you ready to leave, or . . ."

Pike slid his arms around her and pressed her to him. "What do *you* think?" he said with a smile.

He rolled her over so that she was on her back and began to kiss and suck her breasts until the nipples were hard as little pebbles. She moaned and ran her fingers through his hair as his head moved lower, until finally his face was nestled between her legs. He licked her, getting his face wet, and used his elbows to pin her thighs to the bed. He continued to work on her with his tongue until her legs tensed and her belly began to tremble. She tried to move, but he had her pinned, and that seemed to intensify the sensations that were coursing through her. Finally she gave a muffled cry.

Pike wondered how many times a whore had cried out in mock pleasure in this brothel, and wondered too if the other whores could tell whether Colette was acting or not.

He chose to believe that she was not.

Colette watched with pleasure as Pike dressed.

"Will you be coming back?" she asked.

"I'll be leaving in the morning."

She shrugged. "That still leaves tonight. Where were you planning on sleeping?"

"I'm sharing a tent with a friend."

"Where was *he* intending to sleep?"

He looked down at her and said, "That has yet to be

55

worked out."

"Well," she said, "work it out and let me know."

"Are we talking about a business arrangement?" he asked.

She smiled coyly. "That has yet to be worked out."

Chapter Six

Pike was walking past Ted Clark's when McConnell came out with the entire Russian party. Koloff seemed to be in a very happy mood.

"Ah, Pike, there you are," he said, spreading his arms expansively. "You will be pleased to know that I have commissioned Sun Rising to come along with us to do the cooking."

"Sun Rising?" Pike said. He cast a glance at McConnell, who shrugged. "What about Vanya?"

Koloff laughed and looked at Vanya.

"Vanya has many talents," he said, still laughing, "but I can assure you that cooking is not one of them."

Pike looked at Vanya, who only smiled.

Koloff said something to his men in Russian, and all but Colonel Makarov left to escort the ladies back to their tent. It was then that Pike noticed that Charles Severance was not present.

"Ivan," Pike said, "how does Vanya feel about Sun Rising coming along?"

"Do you mean, is she jealous?"

Pike nodded.

"You may not have noticed, but the two women have become very good friends," Koloff said. "Before deciding to commission Sun Rising as our cook, I was going to bring her along as Vanya's companion. Now she may act as both."

"I see."

"Do you have any objection?"

"I suppose not," Pike said. "If the Crow don't want her I guess they won't bother us if she's along."

"Excellent!" Koloff said. He placed his hand on Pike's shoulder and said, "You're my guide and I want to keep you happy. If you don't want her along, we will not take her."

Pike stared at Koloff for a few moments, then shook his head. "It makes no difference to me whether she comes or not."

"Good," Koloff said. "Then she'll come." Koloff pointed at the trading post and said, "Mr. McConnell introduced us to your friend's wife and her wonderful stew. I've never tasted anything like it. Have you had some?"

"Yes," Pike said, "but I think I'll go inside for something to drink."

Koloff turned to McConnell and said, "I will send back one of my men to help you with the supplies."

"I could use Leonid," McConnell suggested.

"I will send him."

Koloff nodded to them both, then turned and walked away.

"Leonid is a pretty decent sort," McConnell explained to Pike as they watched Koloff walk off.

"I know," Pike said.

"I'm not too sure about Koloff, though," McConnell continued. "I can't really read him well."

"I know," Pike said again. "Coming inside for a drink?"

"I'll be in for the supplies shortly," McConnell replied. "I want to stow them before we turn in."

"I'll see you inside then."

Pike mounted the steps and entered the trading post. Charles Severance was seated at one of the tables nursing a beer. Clark looked up at him from behind the bar and Pike held up one finger.

"One beer, comin' up," Clark said.

Pike walked over to Severance and asked, "Mind if I join you?"

Severance looked up and shrugged. Pike sat opposite him. He studied the man for a moment. Severance was a slight man in his thirties, with smooth skin, even on his hands. It appeared that Charles Severance had never done a difficult day's work in his life.

"What did you do to get sent here?" Pike asked.

Severance looked up at him again and then laughed. There was no humor in the sound.

"Let's just say I fell out of favor with the powers that be," Severance said. "They tried to think of the most distasteful job they could come up with for me, and believe me, they succeeded."

"A guide?"

"An escort," Severance corrected. "An official government escort. I couldn't be anyone's guide, Pike. I don't know my way around this world." When he said *this world* he held his arms out to encompass everything that was around them. "I'd be lost without *them*." He gestured in the general direction of the Russians.

Clark came over and put a beer down in front of Pike, who thanked him.

"How long will this go on?"

Severance shrugged and said, "Until Koloff gets homesick, I guess."

"He looks to be having too much of a good time for that," Pike remarked.

"Sure," Severance said. "Everyone has a good time except for old Charlie Severance."

"Why not?"

Severance looked at Pike and asked, "Why not what?"

"Why not have a good time?"

"Here?"

59

"Why not? What good are you doing feeling sorry for yourself?"

"No good," Severance said, "no good at all."

"Then enjoy yourself, Charles," Pike said. "Have some fun."

"In this godforsaken place?"

"There's a place to enjoy yourself, even here," Pike said. "Do you like women?"

Severance laughed his humorless laugh again.

"The only woman I've seen for months has been Vanya, and she belongs to Koloff."

"Now there's Sun Rising," Pike said with a grin.

Severance looked appalled.

"An Indian girl? Never!"

"How about a nice white girl, then?" Pike asked. "To enjoy yourself with?"

"Where?" Severance asked.

"Finish your drink," Pike said, "and I'll take you there."

Pike walked Severance over to the whorehouse. The madam approached him and said, "Back again so soon?"

"My friend is looking for some enjoyment in life," Pike replied, pushing Severance forward a few steps.

"Well," the madam said, "if he can't find it here he won't find it anywhere. What size, color, and shape enjoyment did you have in mind?"

Severance swallowed hard and asked, "What size, color, and shapes do you have?"

"Honey, I've got everything," she said, laughing.

"You discuss it with him," Pike remarked, "and see that I get the bill."

"Pike—" Severance said, starting to object.

"Never mind, Charles," Pike said. "This is my home ground, and I'm showing you where to find the enjoyment. When I'm on your home ground, you can foot the bill. All right?"

Severance smiled, and this time it was real.

"All right," he said, "it's a deal."

Pike watched while the madam took Severance's arm and walked him away, then turned and left.

Pike helped McConnell and Leonid carry the supplies to the livery, then he and McConnell went back to Ted Clark's for another drink.

Clark's was busy now. Sky Woman was nowhere to be seen, because when the place filled with men she stayed in the back.

The tables were all taken, so Pike and McConnell took up a position at the bar.

"Why did you take him there?" McConnell asked after Pike told him what he had done with Severance.

"I don't know," Pike said. "He looked so miserable sitting there by himself, crying into his beer."

"And it wouldn't hurt to have a representative of the government in your debt, eh?"

Pike smiled and said, "Yeah, that too."

"Well," McConnell said, "After I finish this beer I might just go over there and join him."

"Go over there," Pike said, "but get your own girl."

"You know what I mean," McConnell said, grimacing.

"Yeah, I know what you mean," Pike said. "Will you be coming back to the tent tonight?"

McConnell looked at Pike and asked, "Why? Do you have some plans?"

"I'd just like to know."

"Well," McConnell said thoughtfully, "it wouldn't put too much of a strain on my purse to spend the night. The tent is yours."

Pike nodded.

McConnell leaned forward and asked his friend, "Which is it to be? Vanya or Sun Rising?"

"Neither."

McConnell sat back, finished his beer, and then stood up.

"Well, whoever it is, have a pleasant night. I'll see you in the morning."

Pike waved and McConnell went to the door and left.

"Another?" Clark asked.

"Why not?"

Clark brought it and sat opposite Pike.

"When will you be leaving?"

"Tomorrow, first light."

"Going after another bear, huh?"

"I guess."

"Didn't have enough last time?"

"I guess not."

"Any dreams this time?"

"No dreams, Ted," Pike said, "just a lot of money."

"Well, I hope you're gettin' enough to make up for the trouble you're gonna have."

"What trouble?"

"Believe me," Clark said, "that bunch is trouble looking for a place to happen."

Pike reckoned he knew that too, but it seemed to be something he couldn't control. Trouble was going to happen, but he figured that knowing that might make it easier to handle.

Pike left Ted Clark's and walked over to the whorehouse. The madam smiled slyly when she saw him.

"Again?" she asked.

"I'd like to see Colette," Pike said.

A few minutes later the pretty blonde entered the room. She seemed glad to see him.

"I'm going to bed now," Pike told her with a grin.

"Did you come to say good night?"

Pike ignored the question and continued with what he had come to say.

"I have a tent at the far end of the settlement."

"What happened to your friend?"

"He found someplace else to sleep tonight. Someplace nice and warm."

"That was nice of him. How will I tell your tent from the others?"

"I'll leave a light by the door."

"I'll probably be late," she warned.

"I'll be up."

She smiled again and said, "I certainly hope so."

Chapter Seven

When Pike got back to his tent he set a storm lamp down by the entrance, then laid McConnell's blanket out on the floor. That done, he laid his own blanket on top of it, then folded it down halfway. He hoped it wouldn't look too uninviting.

He heard someone outside the tent and looked up just in time to see her enter.

It wasn't Colette.

It was Vanya.

"Good evening," she said, looking down at him. "Were you expecting someone?"

"Vanya!" he said, standing up.

"You were expecting me?"

"No, I wasn't," he said, "but now that you're here I think we should establish some rules for the trip."

She had a shawl wrapped around her shoulders and she was holding it closed in front. Beneath it she wore pants, a shirt, and boots. She looked beautiful.

"What kind of rules?"

"The kind that keep you from coming to my tent at night."

"Why?"

"Because I work for Koloff," Pike said, "and you belong to Koloff."

She frowned and said, "I do not *belong* to Ivan."

"Well, that's the impression I get," Pike said. "What do you call it?"

"I am his . . . companion."

"Okay, you're his companion," Pike said. "That still means that you should stay out of my tent."

"Even if I was sent by Ivan?"

Now it was Pike's turn to frown.

"Koloff sent you here?"

"He did."

"Why?"

"I think the main reason was that he wanted to be alone with Sun Rising."

"And that doesn't bother you?"

"Why should it?"

"Well, you are his companion."

"I work for him," she said, "just as you do. I thought that would give us something in common."

"It does, but—"

"When he tells me to take a walk, I take a walk," she said. "Then when he tells me to take a walk by your tent, that is what I do. Were you?"

"Were I what?"

"Expecting someone?"

Guiltily, Pike looked down at the two blankets he had set out on the floor.

"No."

There were two pallets set up in the tent, courtesy of Koloff's men. She glanced at them and smiled.

"Do you prefer sleeping on the ground?"

"It does have its advantages."

"Like what?"

"Well, for one thing, I can't fall off."

"You're probably used to sleeping on the ground, anyway."

"I don't usually carry a bed around with me, it's

65

true," he said.

She got down on her knees on the blanket and re-moved the shawl.

"It looks as if it would be comfortable."

"That depends."

"On what?"

"On what you plan to do on it."

She looked up at him and began to unbutton her shirt.

"What were you planning to do on it?"

"Sleep."

She peeled the shirt off, exposing her milky white breasts. They were round and firm looking.

"Alone?"

"I had planned on sleeping alone, yes."

"Well," she said, "my presence should not change that." She sat down and began to pull her pants off.

"Why not?"

She discarded her pants, smiled, and said, "I did not come here to sleep."

She was now clad only in a pair of white underwear. She got to her knees once again, rested her hands on her thighs, and looked up at him.

"Would you like to join me?"

Pike joined her, wondering just how late Colette was going to be.

Vanya was expert at lovemaking. When Pike joined her on the blanket she helped him off with his clothes and then slithered down between his legs. She used her mouth and tongue and teeth to bring him to the point of bursting, and then refused to allow him to come. In-stead, she continued to work on him, giving him some pleasure and some pain, until finally she decided it was time. She brought him to an explosion that lifted him up off the ground, reaching for her . . .

After that Pike decided to try to do the same thing to her. He got down between her legs and used his mouth and lips to bring her to the brink of orgasm. Then he reached beneath her, cupped her buttocks, and lifted her off the ground until he brought her to an orgasm that had her writhing beneath him, pounding the blanket with her fists . . .

Pike sat on the blanket, watching her dress. She was once again the cool, collected lady, not at all the writhing, moaning creature she had been just moments earlier.

"Where are you going now?" he asked.

"Back to Ivan's tent."

"Just like that?"

She looked down at herself and then said, "Like what?"

"Never mind. Are you sure Koloff knew you were coming here?"

"Well," she said sheepishly, "maybe he did not know exactly where I was going."

Pike stood up, reaching for his pants, and said, "Maybe we should talk about those rules?"

She smiled at him, licked her lips lasciviously and said, "As far as I am concerned, Pike, there are no rules. Good night."

She left him standing there, his pants in his hand, wishing they had stuck to talking about rules when the subject had first been brought up.

He was also hoping that when Colette said she would be late, she had meant *very* late.

* * *

She did.

In fact, Pike had fallen asleep by the time she arrived. He heard her sliding into the tent and opened his eyes.

"Colette."

She smiled and said, "Were you expecting someone else?"

"No," he said, "definitely not."

Colette had dressed warmly for the walk across the settlement, but she was adept at removing her clothes quickly. In moments she was underneath the blanket with Pike.

"You have your pants on," she said.

"I know."

She unbuckled his pants and helped him take them off, tossing them aside.

"Oooh," she said, rubbing up against him.

Her flesh was hot and her hand was active beneath the blanket. For a moment he wasn't sure he was going to be able to perform again, but Colette quickly saw to that. In just a few moments he had swelled in her educated hand. She slid her thigh over him, rubbing her pubic mound against him, pressing her lips to his chest. He reached for her, pulled her on top of him, and entered her in one swift movement.

"Oh, Jesus . . ." she gasped, and began to ride him . . .

Colette rose and dressed just before first light. Pike watched her, as he had watched Vanya. The women were so totally different—except when they were making love. They were both experienced women who thoroughly enjoyed sex and weren't shy about what they wanted.

In fact, Vanya was as experienced as Colette, who did it for a living, a fact that made Pike wonder about Vanya.

"What are you thinking about?" Colette asked.

Pike started, then looked at her and said, "You."

"Oh?" she said. "We're going to start lying to each other now?"

Pike decided to tell her the truth.

"I was thinking about another woman, and how you and she are so much alike."

"Would that be the dark-haired woman who left here last night before I got here?"

"You saw her?"

"Sure, I saw her," Colette said. "I wasn't as late as I thought I was going to be."

"Then why did you get here so long after her?"

Colette laughed and said, "I had to give you time to recover—and you did, admirably. I don't know many men who could satisfy two women in one night. You say she reminds you of me?"

"She does," Pike said. "In a lot of ways you're very much alike."

"In bed?"

"Yes."

"Then I *am* impressed. Is she your woman?"

"No."

"Whose?"

"The man I work for."

Colette frowned and said, "That doesn't sound like the right way to start a new job."

"It isn't," he agreed, "but then it wasn't my idea."

Colette had finished dressing and now she smiled down at him.

"She sounds like a woman who knows what she wants and how to get it."

"She is."

"Then it sounds like you'd better be very careful over the next few weeks."

"I'll take your advice and be careful."

She leaned over and kissed him.

"Bye, lover," she said. "See you when you come back this way again. Soon, I hope."

When Pike left the tent he saw McConnell coming his way.

"And how was your night?" McConnell asked.

"Tiring," Pike retorted, "and yours?"

"Eventful. Well," he said, looking past Pike, "they're prompt."

Pike turned and saw two of Koloff's men. They had apparently come to take down the tent.

"Let's get our gear," Pike said. "I want to be ready when they are."

"These guys might be hard to keep up with," McConnell remarked.

Pike looked up at the high peaks and said, "Not up there. Up there *we're* the ones who are going to be hard to keep up with."

"If there's no bear up there," McConnell said, "it's going to be a very long trip."

"There'll be a bear," Pike said.

McConnell looked at him and said, "Dream?"

"No," Pike replied, "no dream. Just a hunch."

"What else does your hunch tell you?"

"Let's go and collect our gear and animals," Pike said, "and I'll tell you."

Part Two
Bear Hunt

Chapter Eight

By the time Pike and McConnell had their gear collected and stowed onto two mules—also purchased from Ted Clark—Koloff and his party were packed and ready to go.

Pike watched as Charles Severance mounted his horse. Severance saw Pike looking at him and nodded, smiling. The man probably had a lot to smile about this morning, but Pike couldn't help wondering how long that would last. Severance seemed to be more accustomed to frowning . . .

There was no way they could make good time. The Russians had so much gear that they needed five mules to carry it all. Nevertheless, even trailing seven mules in all, they still made pretty decent progress before Pike called a halt for lunch.

"Can't we keep moving?" Koloff asked.

"Mules are beasts of burden, Ivan," Pike said, "but even they need a rest. We'll have some coffee and rest a while and then continue."

Koloff agreed, bowing to Pike's superior experience in such matters.

Sun Rising knew nothing about coffee, so Leonid prepared it, showing her how it was done. She was pretty smart and wouldn't need to be shown again.

73

Sitting at the fire with Pike and McConnell, Koloff asked, "How soon will it be before we can start looking for the bear?"

"That depends," Pike said.

"On what?"

"On whether we're looking for the bear," McConnell piped in, "or he ends up looking for us."

"I would like very much for him to come looking for us," Koloff said, touching his rifle. "I will be ready for him."

"Talk about being ready," Pike said, "I've been thinking about something since we left this morning."

"What?"

"The tents." Pike said. "I wish I had thought of this before we left."

"Thought of what?" Koloff asked impatiently.

"Do we really need all these tents?" Pike asked.

"Well . . ." Koloff said, thoughtfully, "I suppose we could do with fewer tents. You and McConnell would have to sleep in the open . . ."

"We prefer sleeping in the open."

"I suppose my men could sleep outside . . . and Sun Rising, I'm sure she's used to it."

"That leaves Severance, you, and Vanya."

Koloff laughed and said, "Mr. Severance does not seem to be the outdoor type."

"I think he'll be fine sleeping outside," Pike said. "What about you and Vanya?"

Koloff looked surprised.

"Me?" Koloff seemed shocked. "Pike, I really would prefer to keep my tent. Why are the tents a problem, anyway?"

"Well, for one thing, we wouldn't need as many mules if we dumped the tents."

"What would we do with them?"

"The mules or the tents?"

"Both."

"We could just dump the tents and release the mules. They'd find they're way back to the settlement."

"You said that was one reason," Koloff said. "There are others?"

"Probably a lot of them, but the one that comes to mind is this. With all the tents it makes it hard to break camp in a hurry."

"Why would we have to?"

"Lots of reasons," McConnell said, "but the most important are Indians or bear."

"Well, if that should occur," Koloff said, "I mean, if we should have to, uh, break camp, as you say, we could leave the tents behind then, couldn't we?"

"Yes, we could," Pike said, "but—"

"That settles it, then," Koloff said, standing up. "We will keep the tents until it becomes absolutely necessary to dump them."

"Well, if it's all the same to you," Pike said, "Skins and I will sleep outdoors. And I suspect Sun Rising will also."

"That remains to be seen," Koloff said, with a smile, "but you and Mr. McConnell may do as you wish."

"We'll have to set watches, too," Pike said.

"You can use my men for that."

"We'll split them," Pike continued. "There are enough of us that the same men won't have to stand watch every night."

"Well," Koloff said, somewhat stiffly, "as long as you do not expect me to stand watch."

"You?" Pike said, feigning surprise. "Why would I expect you to do that?"

Koloff didn't notice the sarcasm in Pike's voice, either that or he simply ignored it.

Pike doused the fire while McConnell collected the pot and cups and gave them to Leonid to stow away.

That done, they all remounted and started off again, the mules being led by Koloff's men—all except Colonel Makarov. The bodyguard kept both hands free at all times.

From observing the man, Pike suspected that the colonel was probably very good at his job.

By nightfall they had not come across any bear tracks, but Koloff had again proved himself an excellent marksman when he took down a running deer with one shot. Pike had been ready to back the man up in case of a miss, but it had not been necessary.

When they camped for the night Pike watched as Sun Rising expertly skinned and cut the deer and with Leonid's help set the entire torso on a spit to cook. She also made a huge pot of coffee, demonstrating that she needed to be shown how to do something only once.

Pike and McConnell did not help set up the tents. Even more than before, Pike disliked the idea of having them up. To a passing party of Crow or Blackfoot, the tents might make the difference between a decision to attack or simply to pass on. The tents were like a sign that said: "This camp has much to offer."

Before long the camp was filled with the scent of cooking meat, and if that didn't attract the attention of a bear in the area, nothing would.

Pike remembered his last experience with a bear. He had dreamed about the beast and had finally come face to face with it. His friends McConnell and Whiskey Sam had fired on the bear, but even gravely wounded it still managed to grab hold of Pike and lift him off his feet. Pike had killed it by jamming his Kentucky pistol under the animal's huge slavering jaw and firing, driving a lead ball into the creature's brain.

He rubbed his ribs, remembering the pressure of the

bear's paws.

"What are you thinking about?" McConnell asked.

"Bears."

"All bears," McConnell asked, "or one bear in particular?"

"One in particular."

"Let's hope we don't run into one like that again."

The bear in question had been huge, more than enough to satisfy a man like Koloff. Pike too hoped that, if and when they did find Koloff a bear, it would not be one of that size and ferociousness.

Chapter Nine

In the morning Pike was the first to rise.

Koloff's three men had split the watch that first night. On the second night Pike intended that he, McConnell, and Makarov would take the watches. He was interested to see how Makarov would react.

Pike had the coffee going by the time Sun Rising arose, only seconds ahead of Leonid's appearance from inside his tent.

"I will start breakfast," Sun Rising said, squatting on the other side of the fire.

"All right," Pike replied, moving away.

He was bare-chested, and Sun Rising watched him for a few moments before beginning breakfast.

"What can I do?" Leonid asked.

"Check with your countryman on watch," Pike said. "Make sure he's all right, and then check the horses."

Leonid nodded and went to take care of it. He seemed eager to do his part. In fact, all of the Russians seemed willing to do their part—all except Koloff himself, but then he was paying the freight, wasn't he? Pike hadn't tried to give Makarov a job yet. That would come tonight, when they made camp.

McConnell was the next to rise, scratching his head and squinting at the sun.

"I smell coffee," he said.

"It's ready," Pike called.

McConnell shivered and said to his friend, "Put on a damned shirt, will you? You're making me feel even colder than I am."

Pike smiled, but he put on his shirt. Leonid returned and said that the horses were all fine.

"You might want to wake the others, then," Pike suggested.

Leonid executed a small bow and went off to do just that.

"Skins, let's have a look around the camp."

"For what?" McConnell asked over a steaming cup of coffee.

"Tracks."

"What kind?"

Pike stared at McConnell for a moment, then said, "Any kind. Take the coffee with you if you want."

"All right, all right," McConnell said, "I'm coming."

"I'll work my way around this way," Pike said, making a motion with his finger, "and you go that way."

"Sounds fair to me."

As Pike started to walk away Sun Rising appeared before him with a cup of coffee.

"Coffee?"

"Uh, when I come back, Sun Rising."

She nodded, and moved out of his way.

He could already smell the cooking bacon.

Pike made his half circle around the camp and found no sign that anyone had approached during the night. There were no tracks of any kind to be seen.

When he returned to the fire, McConnell reported the same.

"Breakfast?" Sun Rising said, holding out a plate of bacon.

"Yes, thank you, Sun Rising."

79

"Coffee," she said, handing him a cup.

"Thanks."

She held his eyes for a moment with hers, then returned to the fire and started handing out plates and cups to the others.

Leonid took a plate and a cup of coffee and said, "I'll take this in to him."

Him, of course, was Koloff.

"What about Vanya?" Pike asked.

Leonid stopped and looked over his shoulder at Pike long enough to say, "She will come out for hers," and then continued on.

McConnell looked at Pike and said, "I guess Koloff is the only one who gets served breakfast in bed around here, eh?"

"I guess so," Pike said. His dislike for the man he was working for was growing. He hoped they found him a bear real soon.

Soon enough Vanya appeared and Sun Rising handed her her breakfast. Vanya thanked her and found herself a place to sit right next to Pike. Everyone was now present, except for Koloff.

"Did you sleep well under the stars?" she asked.

"I always do."

"The cold did not bother you?"

"It rarely does."

"Pike likes the cold," McConnell said. "Whenever we're camped out near a lake he takes a dip every morning, no matter how cold it is."

"Really?" Vanya said. "You must have some Russian blood in you, yes?"

Pike laughed and said, "No, I don't think so. Is your country cold?"

"Very cold," she said, smiling. "I think you would be

very at home there, no?"

"I don't know," Pike said. "I guess you would be the best judge of that, wouldn't you?"

"I think that I would, yes." .

She took a deep breath and said, "I love the way the air feels in my lungs."

"Yes," Pike said, "I love it also."

"You know," she remarked, "I don't think I have felt so alive since my arrival in your country as I do in your mountains."

"They're not my mountains," Pike said.

"Don't believe him, ma'am," McConnell said. "These *are* his mountains. He's made them his mountains."

Pike was about to reply when Ivan Koloff put in his appearance. Pike thought that Koloff would probably appear last every morning, just so he could command everyone's attention.

"What a morning!" he announced, making a show of taking a deep breath and rubbing his chest. "These mountains are marvelous!"

Pike couldn't argue with that, so he chose not to reply.

"I see you are all almost finished with your breakfast," Koloff announced.

No sooner had he said that than his men all put down their plates. Vanya followed suit just seconds later, even though Pike, seated right next to her, could see that she was far from finished.

The Russians rose and walked to their tents to get ready to leave.

Severance, unsure of what to do, finally put his plate down and said, "I, uh, better get my things ready to, uh, leave . . ."

Sun Rising looked across the fire at Pike, frowning. She had served everyone else before preparing a plate for herself and was also far from finished.

"Finish eating, Sun Rising," Pike said. "There's no reason for you to stop."

Sun Rising looked from Pike to Koloff, who was staring at her.

"It does not matter," she said to Pike. "I will start to clean up."

She put her plate down and McConnell picked it up.

"If she's not going to finish it, I am," McConnell said.

Pike looked at Vanya's plate, then picked it up and scraped it off into his. He and McConnell were the guides, and he was damned if anyone was going to make them rush their breakfast. The others could scurry about at Koloff's whim, preparing to leave simply because he announced himself ready, but no one was leaving until Pike and McConnell were finished eating.

Koloff was about to learn that.

When Pike and McConnell had finished, McConnell helped Sun Rising clean up while Pike collected their gear and tied it to their mules. That done, he saddled first his horse and then McConnell's, taking his own sweet time about it.

Truth be told, Pike would have liked to be under way earlier, but the way the Russians, Sun Rising, and Severance, reacted to Koloff's orders, even foregoing their breakfasts simply because *he* was ready to leave, stuck in his craw.

Pike knew that Koloff was watching him, but he refused to turn and look at the man. He knew that in a way he was being childish, but he had to prove a point. He also knew his attitude was going to lead to the two of them butting heads eventually, but he was actually looking forward to that.

Slowly Pike led the horses over to where McConnell was stomping out the fire. When McConnell was done, Pike handed him his reins.

"Are you ready to leave, Mr. McConnell?" Pike asked.

"I'm ready," McConnell said. "Are you ready, Mr. Pike?"

"Oh, I think I'm ready."

They looked behind them to where all the others were ready and waiting, in fact, had been waiting for some time.

"Are we all ready?" Pike asked.

Koloff knew what Pike and McConnell were doing. He nodded, executing a slight bow, and said, "We are ready when you are, Mr. Pike."

"Good," Pike said, "let's move out."

Chapter Ten

By midday they had reached snow.

"Now," Koloff said, "this truly does remind me of my country, eh, Vanya?"

"Yes, Ivan."

McConnell leaned over and in a low voice said to Pike, "I think you really would be at home in their country."

"Not if there are a lot of men like him," Pike said.

"What about women like her?"

"Every country must have its good and bad points, Skins."

"Well, she certainly does have two good points that I can see."

"Just remember who those two points belong to," Pike reminded him.

"She doesn't seem to think they belong to anyone in particular," McConnell said. "Not the way she keeps looking at you."

Pike and McConnell were riding point, so there was no danger of them being heard by the others. On the other hand, they could hear the rest of the party very well.

Koloff and Makarov had their heads together and were speaking Russian. Pike found that odd since Koloff had been demanding of his people that they speak only English. What was it Koloff could have to say to his bodyguard that he didn't want Pike and McConnell to understand?

Further back Pike could hear the voices of Sun Rising and Vanya. Sun Rising seemed to be giving Vanya lessons on living in the mountains.

"Why don't you just concentrate on Sun Rising," Pike suggested. "You wanted her bad enough a few days ago."

"I learned my lesson," McConnell said. "Koloff seems to consider her his private property, her *and* Vanya."

"Why don't you ask her what she thinks?"

"She thinks she wants you, just like Vanya," McConnell said. "Face it, Pike, that big body of yours is just irresistible to women, no matter where they come from."

"If that's the case," Pike said, "I'll trade bodies with you."

"You won't fare any better with mine," McConnell said with a wide grin. "I appeal to certain women too."

"Unfortunately, none of them seem to be along on this trip."

"Look," Pike said suddenly, reigning his horse in and jerking his chin ahead of them.

McConnell turned his head and looked where Pike was indicating.

"Crow?" McConnell asked.

"Blackfoot."

"Trouble?"

"We'll have to see."

"What's the problem?" Koloff asked, riding up alongside of Pike.

"Indians," McConnell replied.

"How marvelous," Koloff said. "Where?"

"Straight ahead."

85

Koloff looked and asked, "How many of them are there?"

"They're letting us see about half a dozen," Pike said.

"If that is all they number then we have the advantage," Koloff said.

Pike looked at Koloff and said, "You never have the advantage when it comes to Indians. There could be thirty or forty others that we can't see."

"Where can they be?" Koloff asked, striking an exaggerated pose and looking around. "I do not see them."

"That's the point," Pike said. "You won't see them until they want you to."

"So what are we to do?" Koloff asked. "Wait here until they attack us?"

"They might not attack us," Pike said. "Let's just wait and see what they want."

"That's nonsense," Koloff said. He turned in his saddle and barked out something in Russian. Leonid turned and relayed the order, and the other three men broke formation and rode up to Koloff. Severance, further back, looked worried. Makarov, sitting on his horse right behind Koloff, kept his face expressionless.

Koloff started to speak to his three men in Russian when Pike broke in, "English!"

"I beg your pardon?" Koloff asked, turning his head slowly in Pike's direction.

"What are you telling them?"

"I am instructing them to ride ahead and disperse those savages."

"Oh, no," Pike said, "no way."

"Mr. Pike," Koloff said, "I was under the impression that I was in command here."

"Then you're under the wrong impression," Pike said. "You hired me to guide you, that means you do what I tell you."

"That was not our—"

"It's either that or McConnell and I turn around right now and go back the way we came."

Koloff stared at Pike with a stony expression.

"What's it going to be, Ivan?"

They matched stares a little longer, McConnell turning in his saddle to keep an eye on Makarov. Finally, Koloff looked at his men and curtly said something in Russian. They turned and rode to the back of the line.

"We will do it your way," Koloff said, and then added, "This time."

Pike ignored the remark.

"Already they've probably found us very interesting," Pike said. "We were arguing amongst ourselves, and we have two women with us, one of which is a Crow squaw."

"What are they likely to want from us?" Koloff asked.

"Oh, some food," Pike said, "some whiskey, if we had any, and probably Sun Rising."

"We will give them some food," Koloff said, "but I will not part with Sun Rising."

Pike looked at Koloff, who seemed adamant.

"She warming your blankets, yet?"

"I beg your—"

"Just answer my question, Ivan!" Pike said.

Koloff squared his chin and shoulders and said, "Of course—"

"Don't lie to me," Pike said. "You telling me the truth could mean the difference between us being killed or getting out of here alive."

Koloff considered that for a moment and then said, "No, she has not yet . . . warmed my blankets, as you say."

"And you want to keep her until she does."

"Yes."

"You might pay a high price to keep her, Ivan," Pike

87

said.

"I am already paying *you* a high price," Koloff pointed out. "As you have said, it's up to you to get us out of here, no?"

"Yes," Pike said, "it is."

Pike turned to McConnell and said, "Keep the others here."

"Right."

Pike made a show of handing McConnell his rifle and his Kentucky pistol, and then began to ride toward the half-dozen Blackfoot braves.

"What does he think he can do without weapons?" Koloff asked.

"Why don't we just wait and see?"

As Pike approached the braves one of them spoke.

"You are He-Whose-Head-Touches-the-Sky," the brave said.

Pike had only recently become aware that the Indians in the area—Crow, Blackfoot, Snake—had begun calling him that. He was not displeased by it, although to him being tall was no special feat. It had sort of happened to him without any help.

"I am."

The brave looked past Pike to the others.

"You have two women."

"We do."

"We want one."

"We have food we can let you have, and perhaps some supplies."

"And a woman," the brave said.

Pike had been looking carefully about and had satisfied himself that these six braves were alone. That meant he might be able to bluster his way through. They were nine men and two women against six braves.

That was as slight an advantage as you could have, but it was an advantage all the same.

"No woman."

"But you have two."

"They are not mine," Pike said, "or I would give you one."

"Who do they belong to?"

"Others in my party."

"We will fight for them."

Pike shook his head.

"We will not fight for what is already ours. We offer you food and supplies."

The brave thought it over, then said, "What supplies?"

"Blankets."

"And food?"

"Bacon, some venison."

The brave turned and spoke in low tones to the others.

"We will forego the supplies for one woman. One woman only."

Pike started to turn his horse, saying, "If we cannot come to an agreement then we will simply go on—"

"Wait!"

Pike stopped, his horse half turned, and waited, not looking at the man.

"We will take the food and supplies," the brave said, "and one mule."

Pike held back a smile. He was willing to bet that they had wanted a mule all along and had simply used the demand for a woman as a ploy.

"Wait," he said, and rode back to his party.

"Well?" Koloff asked.

"They want food, blankets, and a mule."

"Not one of the women?"

"They wanted one of the women but they settled for a mule."

Koloff looked confused.

"They can get a woman anywhere."

"And a mule?"

"To them a mule is food."

"They eat mules?"

"And dogs, rats, whatever they can find. An Indian's stomach doesn't care what he puts into it." He turned to McConnell and said, "Pick out a mule. Give them the fattest one."

"Wait," Koloff said. "Why give them the fattest? Why not the worst one?"

"We don't want them coming back to us, do we, Ivan?" Pike said. "We want them to be satisfied." Pike looked at McConnell and said, "Give them the best eating mule."

Koloff made a face as McConnell rode back to pick out the mule. Leonid helped him transfer the mule's burden onto two or three of the other animals, and then McConnell led the mule forward.

While he was doing that Pike was taking some bacon from one of the mules to give to the Indians. When he came to the hunk of deer meat he decided to give them the whole thing. After that he needed only to collect three or four blankets. Luckily, in buying the supplies McConnell had thought to get extras.

They bound up all the supplies for the Indians and secured them to the mule, then Pike mounted up and walked the mule across to them.

The lead brave signaled for one of the others to take the mule, then he nodded to Pike, and they turned and rode away.

Pike considered themselves lucky that the braves had been so easily satisfied.

Of course, that didn't mean they might not come back at some point with reinforcements.

With that happy thought in mind Pike rode back to his party.

"Were they satisfied?" Koloff asked.

"They seemed to be."

"Seemed to be?" Koloff asked. "Mr. Pike, you are the expert on these people. Were they or were they not satisfied?"

Pike gave Koloff a hard stare and said, "They seemed to be."

Koloff stared back at Pike for a few moments, then wheeled his horse around and rode back to his bodyguard.

When they were under way again McConnell said, "If your relationship with Koloff continues to develop the way it has, this could be a long trip."

Pike couldn't have agreed more.

Chapter Eleven

When they camped that night Koloff did not come out of his tent for dinner. Leonid brought it in to him instead, and when Koloff was finished, brought out the empty plate and cup.

"What's on your boss's mind tonight?" McConnell asked Leonid when he returned to the fire.

"I do not know."

"Don't give me that," McConnell said. "You know everything that goes on in that man's head."

Leonid looked up at McConnell and said, "Not everything."

McConnell studied Leonid for a few minutes, then leaned over and tapped him on the shoulder.

"Don't stare into the fire," he said when Leonid looked at him. "It destroys your night vision."

Leonid looked out at the night for a moment, then back at McConnell.

"I understand."

Pike carried his coffee over to where Colonel Makarov was sitting, only a few feet from Koloff's tent.

Pike wondered just what Makarov was colonel of.

As Pike approached the man looked up from his meal. His face was very flat — flat forehead, flat cheeks, even his mouth looked flat. His eyes, however, were sharp, sharp *and* piercing.

"Yes?" he said.

"Watch tonight," Pike said. "You, me, and McConnell. Which would you prefer, first middle, or last?"

The man stared at Pike for a few moments, and Pike thought he was going to refuse.

Instead he said, "Middle."

"Fine," Pike said. "Ill take the first, and then wake you."

"There will be no need for you to wake me."

"Fine," Pike said, "fine . . . I'll see you later, then. We'll take three-hour watches."

The man nodded and went back to his meal without further comment.

Pike walked back toward the fire, saw that McConnell and Leonid were deep in conversation, and altered his course. He found himself walking toward Severance.

"Good evening," Severance said, looking up from his plate.

"Mind if I sit a spell?" Pike asked.

"No, not at all."

Pike sat down next to him on the ground.

"If you don't mind my saying . . ." Severance started, but he trailed off.

"I don't mind," Pike said. "Say what you like."

"Well . . . you don't talk like a mountain man. I mean, you appear to be somewhat . . . educated."

"I had some education as a child," Pike said. "You see, I grew up in the East and came west when I was old enough to travel. I ended up here in these mountains, and I wouldn't leave for anything."

Severance looked around and said, "I can see why."

"Can you?"

Severance looked at him.

"It surprises me, also," he said, "but yes, I can. It's beautiful up here. Pure . . . Life seems fairly simple. You have to look out for Indians and for bears and other animals, but I imagine they would come right at you, wouldn't they?"

"For the most part."

"Where I live, in the city, very few people come right at you."

"I can see where that would be hard to take."

"Ah, but it isn't," Severance said. "Once you've done it awhile you find that you can generally tell what people are going to do, what direction they're going to come at you from."

"I imagine you must be as much an expert in your environment as I am in mine."

"Yes," Severance said, "yes, I am. That is all the more reason I feel out of place here."

"Don't," Pike said. "Just relax, and don't do anything McConnell or I don't tell you to do. You'll get along just fine."

"Would you like me to take a turn on watch?" Severance asked.

Pike started to say no, then decided against it.

"Maybe tomorrow night," he said instead. "Tonight's watches are set."

"All right."

Pike saw the man look past him and turned to see that Vanya had come out of Koloff's tent. Sun Rising was seated at the fire, across from where McConnell and Leonid were talking.

94

Pike thought she was going to walk to Sun Rising, but instead she started toward him.

"I think I'll turn in," Severance said. He got to his feet and said, "Excuse me," then went to the fire to deposit his plate and cup before retiring to his tent.

"Did I scare him away?" Vanya asked. She seated herself on the rock Severance had just vacated.

"You did," Pike said, "but I imagine you're used to that."

"Used to what?"

"Scaring men."

She laughed and said, "Is that what you think I do?"

"Yes."

"Do I scare you?"

"Yes."

"Liar."

He didn't comment, just kept staring at her. There was a three-quarter moon, and its light made her pale skin seem to glow.

"You're very beautiful," he said, "but of course you know that."

"Thank you."

There was an awkwardness between them, as if they had never had sex together back at Clark's Fork. Neither of them had mentioned it since then.

"I guess your boss is having some trouble with Sun Rising."

"Did he tell you that?"

"Sort of."

"I'm surprised," she said. "Ivan does not usually brag about his failures."

"Well, he didn't exactly *brag* about it. Why is he having so much trouble getting her to, uh—"

"Don't you know?"

"How would I know?"

"I would have thought it was fairly obvious that Sun Rising prefers you."

"Did she tell you that?"

"She did," Vanya said, "but she didn't have to. I can see the way she looks at you."

"How's that?"

"The same way I look at you," she said, putting a hand on his shoulder. "We talk about you, you know."

"Not so that Ivan can hear, I hope."

"You are not afraid of Ivan."

"No, I'm not," Pike said, "but that doesn't mean I want to antagonize him, either."

"You fascinate him, you know."

"Do I?"

"Most men are afraid of him."

"Makarov isn't."

"Oh yes, he is," she said, "he just does not allow it to show."

"He hides it very well, then."

"You, on the other hand, clearly are not afraid of him, and you are not impressed by him."

"And this fascinates him?"

"Well that, and it angers him."

"I guessed that I was not one of his favorite people," Pike said wryly.

"And he is not one of yours."

"Is it that obvious?"

"Yes."

"Guess I'm not so good at hiding my feelings as the colonel is."

"He also knows that Sun Rising wants you . . . and that I want you."

"This seems to be getting worse and worse."

"Pike," she said, squeezing his shoulder, "I came over here to warn you."

"About what? Koloff?"

"Yes," she said. "As the days go by he will become more and more . . . jealous of you."

"Jealous? Why, because of you?"

"No," she said, smiling, "but you are thought of in these mountains as he is at home. He is not used to being . . . how would you put it . . . second best."

"Maybe bagging a bear will make him feel different."

"I do not think so."

"Are you suggesting—"

"All I am suggesting is that you be careful. Watch both Ivan and the colonel."

Pike looked over at Makarov, who was watching them openly and without pretense.

"Just how far would the colonel go for Koloff?" Pike asked.

"He would do anything for him," she said. "Anything."

She squeezed his shoulder again, then stood up and walked to the fire to talk to Sun Rising.

Sitting alone, Pike wondered about Vanya. Had she come to him on her own or had Koloff sent her? If Makarov would do anything Koloff told him, what about Vanya? Would she do whatever Koloff told her?

And if so, why would Koloff send her to warn him?

Games, Pike thought. Koloff seemed to be a man who liked games—dangerous games, like cat-and-mouse.

Was he simply trying to give Pike something to think about? Something to worry about? If that was the case, then the man was making a serious mistake.

Pike's mind was never as sharp as when he was worried. It was how he stayed alive.

He stood up and walked to the fire. Leonid had walked away, leaving McConnell alone. As he joined his friend he saw Vanya and Sun Rising rise and walk to the edge of camp, where they sat down, talking.

"Wonder what those two are talking about," he said to McConnell.

"You."

"Maybe that's what I'm supposed to think."

"What do you mean?"

Pike relayed his conversation with Vanya and McConnell listened with interest.

"Well," McConnell said when he was finished, "whatever her reasons for telling you this, I think it's good advice. Why don't I watch Makarov so that you can concentrate on watching Koloff?"

"Good idea," Pike said. "Speaking of watches, Makarov wanted the middle watch. I'll take the first and you the third. All right?"

"Fine."

Pike picked up the coffee pot and poured another cup for McConnell, then one for himself.

"Want to pull out?" McConnell asked.

Pike looked at his friend and scowled.

"That would be the smart thing to do, wouldn't it?" he asked.

"Yup," McConnell said, "but then, neither one us has ever been accused of being smart—well, *real* smart."

Pike stared over at Koloff's tent.

"It's his arrogance that gets to me."

"You put him in his place today with no trouble."

"Yeah, maybe," Pike said, "but he may not back down so easily next time."

"That'll be *his* problem," McConnell said, "won't it?"

"Has it occurred to you how outnumbered we are here?" Pike asked. "I mean, if it came down to that."

McConnell seemed to think about it, counting to himself, and then smiled at Pike and said, "If we can count Sun Rising and Severance on our side, that just might even things up."

"Yeah," Pike said, "it just might."

While Pike and McConnell were sitting at the fire Koloff stuck his head out of his tent and called Makarov inside.

"Sit," Koloff said in Russian. Makarov obeyed.

"What do you think of Pike?" Koloff asked.

"Formidable."

"And his friend?"

"Competent."

"I agree," Koloff said. "I think Pike would be perfect for what I have in mind."

Makarov wasn't sure what this was so he did not comment.

"Tell me, would you feel confident about handling McConnell?"

"Yes."

What else could he say?

"You will watch me, then, for a signal," Koloff said. "Hopefully it will come after we have had our bear, but watch me closely. When the time comes, Mr. McConnell will be your responsibility. Tell the others, if you must—"

"I will not need the others."

"Good," Koloff said, "very good. You can go now, Makarov."

Makarov nodded and left without further word.

When Makarov was gone Koloff sat quite still for a while, still formulating his plan in his head. When he thought he had most of it he rubbed his hands together and thought about Sun Rising. The squaw was not coming to his bed easily, and he was not sure why. Still, he did not want to force her.

Not yet, anyway.

He would give her a little more time to make up her mind. Meanwhile, of course, there was always Vanya . . .

Makarov took up his former position outside the tent. His own tent was pitched right next to Koloff's, within easy earshot. In fact, his tent was always pitched so close that he could hear Koloff and Vanya making love.

Makarov did not like Koloff. He respected him and he obeyed him, but he did not like him. He liked him even less when he heard he and Vanya together. Makarov had never been in love—had never admitted to it, at least—until he met Vanya months ago.

He knew that Koloff was interested in Sun Rising. He also knew that he had not yet taken the squaw to his bed. When he did, he hoped to persuade Vanya to share his tent while Koloff busied himself with the squaw.

Of course, Pike would be a problem. Makarov had seen Vanya go to Pike's tent back at the settlement, and he had watched and waited until she came out again. It was certainly not hard to figure out what they had been doing.

He knew that McConnell was to be his responsibility when the time came—time for what, he did not know yet, but he did not care. He only wished that Koloff had given him Pike instead.

Anyone who looked at Makarov would never suspect the turmoil going on in his mind. Because of his military training, he always managed to present the same facade—cool, cold, calculating.

Inside, however, he was aching to kill someone. And he knew that when he got like that, almost anyone would do . . .

Chapter Twelve

Pike sat his watch contentedly.

Sitting out here, the cold air biting his face and hands, the moonlight making it easy to see, he couldn't have been more content. Skins McConnell was a good friend, the best he'd ever had, but he still valued the time he could spend alone. He wished now that he and McConnell hadn't taken this job, that instead they had split up for a while. Pike would have gone high into the mountains, built himself a lean-to, and spent the time alone. That's what he would do when this was all over, he decided.

He heard someone's foot crunch snow behind him. Whoever it was made no effort to be quiet so he wasn't worried. He didn't even turn.

When she sat next to him he saw that he had been right. From the sound of her footsteps he had known it was Sun Rising. Any of the others—even McConnell—would have made more noise than she had. He was impressed with how quietly she moved. But then again, she was a Crow woman.

"It is a beautiful night," she said.

"Yes, it is."

"You do not mind if I sit with you for a while?"

He hadn't heard her say much up to this point. He

was surprised at how good her English was.

"No, I don't mind."

They sat in silence. Her shoulder was pressed tightly against his, otherwise there was no contact between them.

Finally he looked at her, and she looked back.

"Trouble?" he asked.

"Perhaps," she said.

"Want to talk about it?"

"You know why the Strange One wanted me to come along, don't you?"

It was the first time he had heard her call Koloff "the Strange One," and he thought the name fit.

"I think I do."

"I do not wish to warm his blankets, Pike," she said.

"Have you told him this?"

"No."

"Why not?"

"I think he would . . . kill me."

"I don't think so."

"Why not?"

"Well, for one thing, I wouldn't let him."

She leaned against him even more tightly and let her head drop onto his shoulder.

"I would gladly warm your blankets if you asked me," she volunteered in a small voice.

"I know you would, Sun Rising."

"But you will not ask?"

"I cannot."

"Because of the Strange One?"

"Yes."

"But you are He-Whose-Head-Touches-the-Sky," she said, sounding puzzled. "You are not frightened of him."

"No."

"Then why?"

"I work for him," he said, "I cannot take away what is his."

She sat up straight and said firmly, "But I am not his."

"Tell him that," Pike said, "and then I will take you into my blankets."

"You will?"

Pike told himself No but he heard himself reply, "Yes."

"And you will not let him kill me?"

"No."

Pike knew he was pushing things with Koloff now. The Russian would never believe that he had not put Sun Rising up to this—and in a way he had, hadn't he?

"You and Vanya are friends?"

"Yes."

"Are you sure?"

Sun Rising frowned.

"I think so."

"All right," Pike said. "Go back to bed. Wait until tomorrow night. If he insists that you warm his blankets then you can tell him no, that you . . . you want me."

She put her hands over her mouth and said, "He will be very angry."

"That's all right," Pike said. "Just tell him."

"You will be close?"

"I will be very close by."

"Then I will tell him." She stood up and said, "Good night, Pike."

"Good night, Sun Rising."

He watched her as she walked back to Koloff's tent. She looked over her shoulder at him before entering, and then disappeared.

Pike looked over at Makarov's tent and saw the flap close.

He doubted very much that he was going to have to wake the colonel for his watch.

When his watch was over he stood up and turned in time to see Makarov leave his tent. He waited until the man reached him.

"Remember, three hours," Pike said, "and then wake McConnell."

Makarov nodded and sat down on the stone Pike had just vacated.

Pike walked to his blankets and curled up inside them. He had set his rifle down next to him, but he held the Kentucky pistol beneath the blankets.

Just in case . . .

Makarov could guess what Pike and Sun Rising were talking about. It suited him just fine if Pike stood up to Koloff for the Indian squaw. It might bring things to a head sooner than anyone expected.

Maybe Pike would kill Koloff, and then Makarov would have to kill Pike.

That would leave Vanya free, and in a strange country it would be only natural for her to turn to him.

Pike woke to the smell of coffee. McConnell had started the pot and was sitting at the fire waiting for it to boil.

Pike sat up, tossed aside his blankets, and stood up. He took a moment to tuck the Kentucky pistol into his belt, then he picked up his rifle and joined his friend by the fire.

"What was your talk with Sun Rising about?" McConnell asked.

"What's the matter?" Pike asked. "Couldn't you hear from where you were?"

"Not clearly," McConnell said, "but let me guess. You're going to brace Koloff over her, am I right?"

"The choice is hers."

"I don't think he'll see it that way."

"Maybe not," Pike said. "We'll just have to wait and see."

"Makarov saw the two of you last night."

"I saw him," Pike said. He leaned forward and burned his hand on the pot.

"Careful," McConnell said.

Pike pushed his hand down against the frozen ground.

"Didn't you sleep at all?" Pike asked. "Or were you eavesdropping all night."

"I slept," McConnell said. "Some."

He poured a cup of coffee for Pike and then for himself.

Sun Rising was the next up. She nodded to both of them and busied herself preparing breakfast.

Pike and McConnell stood up and walked with their coffee to the edge of the camp.

"We're getting close," McConnell said.

"I know."

Pike knew that McConnell was referring to the spot where Pike had killed the bear, the bear he had dreamed of. Pike had never been able to figure out what the dream meant or how it had managed to come true. He was just glad that he wasn't dreaming again. He didn't like dreams. He wasn't in control when he was dreaming.

"It's quiet," McConnell said.

"I know."

"Quieter than it needs to be."

"I know that, too."

"There's a bear up here," McConnell said. "If there wasn't, we'd be hearing something—birds or something. I haven't even seen a rabbit."

"Bears tend to clear a wide path," Pike said. "I'm telling you, if we come across another monster—"

"That'll be Koloff's problem, won't it?"

"It may start out that way," Pike said, "but if he can't bring it down alone we'll all have to pitch in."

"Just stay further away from it than you did last time," McConnell said.

"Don't worry," Pike said, rubbing his ribs, "I can still feel the pressure."

Before long everyone was up and eating breakfast. Koloff was less insistent about leaving this morning, and as a result they were on their way earlier than they had been the day before.

Before heading out Pike confided in Koloff what he and McConnell had been discussing.

"So you think we are getting very near?" Koloff asked excitedly.

"I wouldn't be surprised if we ran into a bear today," Pike said. "The only reason I can't say so with certainty is because we haven't seen any physical sign yet."

"Physical sign?"

"Tracks, that kind of thing," Pike said.

"But your instincts tell you he's near," Koloff said. "I would be inclined to put a lot of faith in your instincts,

107

Pike. They seem to be very good."

"They are," Pike said, and then added, "usually."

"I will instruct my men to be alert," Koloff said, "but I will tell them what I am telling you."

"What's that?"

"No one is to shoot," Koloff said. "I will take the bear down myself. Do you understand?"

"Perfectly."

"Good," Koloff said, "then we can get under way very shortly."

"I hope your instincts are right, Pike," McConnell said when Pike joined him. "Back at the settlement Ted Clark told me this group was trouble looking for someplace to happen."

"And?"

"And the suspense is killing me."

Pike knew what his friend meant.

"I don't know why I get myself into these situations," Pike said. "It's clear that I should stay clear of a man like Ivan Koloff."

"It's that competitive streak you have."

"What competitive streak?"

"The one that made you shoot with him and the one that's going to make you vie with him for Sun Rising. That's going to happen tonight, isn't it?"

"What was I supposed to do?" Pike asked. "Let him go on pressuring her, frightening her?"

"Of course not," McConnell said.

"You're damned right, not," Pike said. "No matter who he is, and even if he has a government representative with him, he can't go forcing himself on a woman."

"Definitely not."

Pike saw that his friend was grinning and said, "Oh, shut up!"

"Yes, sir," McConnell said, "I am shutting up as of right now."

Chapter Thirteen

They camped for lunch, and while the others ate, Pike and McConnell walked on ahead to do some scouting.

They hadn't walked a hundred yards when they spotted the tracks.

"There," Pike said, pointing.

"I see it."

They both walked to where the tracks were and bent down to measure them with their hands.

"Big grizzly," McConnell said.

"Just the kind our friend Koloff is looking for," Pike said.

They looked at each other and McConnell said, "Yeah. And just the kind we're not."

"It's a big one, all right."

They stayed in a crouch, both eyeing the tracks with mixed feelings.

"We could . . . take another direction," McConnell suggested.

"No . . ." Pike said thoughtfully, "no, we're taking his money, we're going to have to deliver what he's looking for."

"It's not smart to go after a grizzly this big."

"Maybe it's not," Pike said, standing up. He followed the tracks with his eyes until they disappeared over a rise. "We'd better go back to camp and tell him."

"All right," McConnell said, also standing.

They both stared at the grizzly's tracks for a moment, and then Pike said, "Let's go."

Warily, they retraced their steps back to camp.

Charles Severance watched Koloff and Colonel Makarov, wondering what they were talking so intensely about.

Severance wondered if he should tell Pike about the trouble. Pike had been decent to him; he deserved to know what kind of man Koloff really was.

He deserved to know the danger.

Severance caught Koloff and Makarov looking his way and shivered. He had been warned by both of them after the first two incidents not to speak about them to anyone. Up until now Severance had kept his mouth shut, even though he knew he should have sent telegrams explaining the situation back to Washington.

Severance admitted to himself that he was afraid of both Koloff and Makarov, but maybe Pike was the man to help him.

Maybe Pike could help him get away from this nightmare.

"Look at him," Makarov said to Koloff.

"Do not worry about him," Koloff said. "He is too frightened to do anything."

Makarov looked at Severance with distaste. Severance found something else to look at.

"He is a coward."

"Because he is afraid of us?"

"Because he is afraid."

"Everyone is afraid of something, Colonel," Koloff

said.

"I am not," Makarov said, "and Pike is not."

"No," Koloff said, "I suppose he is not. At least, he has not shown any fear. He might, though, eventually . . ."

Makarov doubted it. Pike was very much like himself: unafraid. He doubted that anything Ivan Koloff could do would frighten a man like Pike.

Pike and McConnell walked back into camp, attracting everyone's attention. Sun Rising stood up and handed them both a cup of coffee.

"Thank you," Pike said. Both men warmed their hands on the cups.

"Did you find anything?" Koloff asked.

Pike hesitated, looking around at their faces, and then said, "Yes, we did."

Koloff stood up.

"What?"

"Tracks."

"Bear tracks?"

Pike nodded.

"Big ones," McConnell said. "This is one big grizzly, Ivan."

"Wonderful!" Koloff said, his face flushing. "How far behind it are we?"

Pike shrugged.

"As cold as it is there's no telling when the tracks were made. We've got a trail to follow now, though, so it shouldn't be long before we catch up to the bear."

"Then let us get started!"

"Simmer down, Ivan," Pike said. "That bear isn't going anywhere. This is its home. Let's finish up here, then we'll break camp and get on its trail."

Koloff stared at Pike for a few moments, then nodded and walked off. He was too impatient to sit down, so he paced.

Makarov studied Pike closely. He saw something in the man's face when he spoke of the bear.

Maybe he was wrong.

Maybe there *was* something that even a man like Pike was frightened of.

When everyone had finished their coffee they broke camp. Pike and McConnell led the way to the grizzly tracks, and Koloff dismounted excitedly to examine them.

"Look at the size of them," he said in a hushed tone. "It must be huge."

"It's big, all right," McConnell said.

Pike watched the faces of the other men in the party as they examined the tracks. Leonid and the other three men did not look happy. True to form, Makarov did not let any expression show as he looked at the tracks.

Sun Rising dismounted and approached the tracks. She got down on her knees and looked closely at the print made by the left hind paw.

"What is it, Sun Rising?" Pike asked.

"Look," she said, pointing.

Pike, McConnell, and Koloff all looked where she was pointing. Pike saw it, an indentation in the center of the paw, as if the animal had a scar from an old wound.

"I see it," Pike said.

"What about it?" McConnell asked.

"I know this bear," she said.

"You've seen it?" Pike asked.

She nodded.

"Is it huge?" Koloff asked.

Sun Rising ignored Koloff and looked at Pike.

"It is very big and it is a killer. It has killed many of my people and it has endured many wounds." She turned her head and looked at Koloff now. "This bear will not die."

"Oh, it will die," Koloff said, cradling his rifle. "It will surely die."

She looked at Pike again as Koloff went back to his horse and mounted up.

"This bear will not die, Pike."

"Sun Rising," Pike said, "you can leave us any time you wish."

"No," she said, "I will stay."

She walked back to her horse and mounted up.

Pike and McConnell stared down at the paw print.

"This bear will not die," McConnell repeated.

"Everything dies, Skins," Pike said. "Don't let her spook you."

"She's not what's spooking me," McConnell said.

Pike knew what he meant.

"Let's get started," Pike said. "The sooner we find this beast the sooner this'll all be over."

McConnell nodded and said, "One way or another."

Chapter Fourteen

Night fell and they still had not caught up with the grizzly. Koloff was displeased and he let everyone know it. He chewed out each and every one of his men, and halfway through dinner Pike heard the sound of a slap. It was unmistakable. Moments later Vanya came out of his tent. She was not holding her face, but there was a red welt on her left cheek.

"Sonofa—" Pike started, getting up.

"You want to get into it tonight?" McConnell asked. "There's still a possibility that you and him are gonna go at it for Sun Rising."

Sun Rising was at the fire preparing dinner, and if she heard she gave no indication.

"Besides which, if you try to get into his tent now you'll have to go through Makarov."

Vanya walked away from the tent toward the edge of camp.

"All right," Pike said. Instead of walking toward the tent he followed Vanya.

When he caught up to her she was holding her cheek. She heard him approach and quickly dropped her hand to her side. Pike took her by the shoulders and turned her around to face him.

"A man who'd hit a woman isn't much of a man in

115

my book," he said.

"Ivan has hit me before."

"And you stay with him?"

"I am in a strange country, Pike," she said. "Without Ivan, I might never get back to my motherland."

"So he hits you and you take it."

"It doesn't happen very often," she said. "He is very frustrated over not catching up to the bear today."

"Once is too often."

She smiled and said, "You want to fight him for me?"

"The mood I'm in, I wouldn't mind."

"You would have to fight Makarov first."

"That wouldn't be a problem."

"He is very formidable."

"So am I," Pike said belligerently.

"Oh, I know," she said. She reached for him, lacing her fingers behind his neck, and pulled his head down to kiss him. At that moment Pike heard something and reacted immediately.

"Look out!" he shouted. He grabbed her around the waist and jumped out of the path of the rushing bear, pulling her with him.

They both hit the ground and the huge brown animal passed very close, ignoring them in his headlong rush into camp.

Pike pulled his Kentucky pistol from his belt and fired into the air to warn the others . . . but it was too late.

The bear attacked with a fury born in hell.

"Stay here!" Pike told Vanya. He had no time to reload his pistol so he just dropped it. His plan was to get to his rifle.

As he entered camp what he saw made him catch his

breath. McConnell, reaching for his rifle, was felled by one swipe of the bear's paw.

Sun Rising managed to avoid the other paw, but went sprawling into the snow anyway.

Koloff's men grabbed their rifles, but by that time the bear was wading into them. He heard them scream as the animal's massive claws tore into their flesh.

Koloff came charging out of the tent to see what was going on, but he hadn't taken his gun with him.

Severance was frozen where he sat, watching as the bear attacked Koloff's men.

Leonid grabbed his rifle, aimed, and fired, but if his shot struck the bear the animal did not react. He tried to reload quickly, but his palsied hands dropped his powder horn.

Pike saw Makarov standing by Koloff's tent, just watching the animal kill his countrymen. Locating his own rifle near the fire he scrambled for it, but by the time he grabbed it the bear had turned away from the men, who were lying motionless on the blood-streaked snow.

The bear stopped and seemed to notice something. It took only a moment for Pike to realize that it was looking at Sun Rising, who was still sitting on the ground.

As Pike raised his rifle to fire, the bear suddenly bolted out of camp and into the darkness. Pike fired, but he could not tell if his shot struck home.

The bear was gone, leaving behind it shock, fear . . . and death.

Pike went to McConnell first.

"You okay?"

McConnell sat up and put his hand to his left shoulder. It came away bloody, but he said, "I'm fine. Check the others."

Pike walked over to Sun Rising, who had risen shakily to her feet.

"Are you all right?"

She didn't answer. Instead she said, "I told you, the bear will not die."

"See to Skins," Pike said. "He's hurt."

"Yes."

Pike went to Koloff's three men, but Leonid was there already.

"They are dead," he said.

It was an understatement. All three men had been torn to pieces. There was a head lying in the snow, a couple of arms and some legs were strewn about, and so much blood had soaked into the snow that it looked pink.

Pike turned toward Koloff's tent. Koloff was standing out front, his rifle in his hands, but Pike was more concerned with Makarov.

He walked over to the colonel, who was still standing.

"What the hell were you doing?"

"I beg your pardon?" Makarov asked.

"You just stood there and watched that bear kill three men—*your* countrymen."

"There was nothing I could do."

"Nothing you could do?" Pike exclaimed. "My God, man, you didn't even raise your rifle. You didn't even try to help them!"

"I could not."

"Why the hell not?"

"He was obeying orders," Koloff said, coming alongside Pike.

"What orders?" Pike asked.

"Don't you remember?" Koloff said. "I gave orders that no one should fire at the beast until I did."

"What?" Pike asked in disbelief. "How the hell could an order like that apply to what just happened here?! Do you even *know* what just happened here? A grizzly, a huge grizzly, attacked a *camp!* It killed three people and you—" he said, turning his attention to Makarov, "—you were concerned about an order?"

"An order is to be obeyed," Makarov said, "no matter what. I need not explain my actions to you."

"It's not your *actions* I'm concerned with, it's your *lack* of action."

"Leonid," Koloff said, looking past Pike, "you fired at the animal?"

"I did."

"Against my orders?"

"Your orders be *damned!*" Pike shouted, standing face to face with Koloff. "Three men are dead and McConnell is hurt. If I hear anything else about *orders* I'm gonna start doing some butt kicking of my own."

Pike turned away from Koloff without waiting for the man's reaction.

"Leonid, these men have to be buried as best we can. Get Severance and start . . . gathering them up."

"At once."

"I'll help as soon as I check on the others."

Leonid nodded, then looked at Koloff before moving. It was only after Koloff nodded that he went to do as Pike said.

Pike walked away from Koloff and Makarov before he could smash their faces in.

McConnell's shoulder was lacerated, but it was not serious. Sun Rising and Vanya, who had returned to camp shocked but unhurt, patched him up.

Pike helped Leonid and a reluctant Severance collect the bodies and wrap them in blankets. Severance had to

119

stop twice to vomit, but to his credit he continued to help—which was more than could be said for Koloff and Makarov. They disappeared inside Koloff's tent and did not reemerge until the bodies had been removed from camp.

Makarov's tent no longer existed. In its flight from the camp the bear had gone right through it.

They recovered the weapons of the three dead men, but none of them could be fired. They were all misshapen, probably from having been trampled, and one was broken cleanly in two.

Finally they carried the bodies away from camp and dug shallow trenches in the snow. They rolled them into the trenches and covered them up as best they could. There was always snow up this high in the mountains, so there was little danger of the bodies ever being unearthed—unless of course some hungry animal dug them up . . .

When they returned to camp Sun Rising had a fresh fire going and had made another pot of coffee. Pike accepted a cup and sat down between Vanya and McConnell.

"How are you doing?" he asked his friend.

"I'll live," McConnell said. He flexed the fingers and gave a bitter grin.

"Will you be able to ride?" Pike asked.

"And shoot," McConnell said. "I want that beast, Pike. He's got a piece of my hide and I want a piece of his."

"You'll have it," Pike promised.

Koloff had approached the fire and heard their exchange.

"Let us not forget, gentlemen, that the bear is mine. No one is to fire—"

"Don't start that shit with me again, Ivan," Pike said tightly. "That bear is fair game. It's killed three men

120

and it came into camp to do it. Do you know how . . . how *unheard* of that is? Right into camp?"

"It is a special beast."

"Yeah," Pike said, laughing bitterly, "that's one way of putting it, all right."

"I warn you," Koloff said. "I will kill that beast myself."

"As long as it's dead," Pike said, "I don't care who kills it."

Koloff stood there for a few moments longer and then barked, "Sun Rising. Come!"

"I need her," Pike said without looking up.

"What?"

Now he looked up.

"I need her," he said again. "She's got to stay with McConnell. His wound could become infected if it's not cleaned regularly."

Koloff considered that, then said, "Vanya—"

"You'll have to go without your pleasures tonight, Ivan," Pike said, interrupting him. "She and Sun Rising will have to take turns watching him."

"This is outrageous—"

"We're going to need his gun, Koloff," Pike said. "We lost three men tonight, and we're going to need all the guns we have to fend off Indians and that bear."

"You think he will attack again?"

"Shit," Pike said, "I never would have expected him to attack the camp the first time, but I don't think he'll be back tonight. He's probably got a burn from running through the fire, and I think Leonid's shot hit him."

"Do you think he might die tonight?" Koloff asked, concerned that he might lose his bear.

"Don't worry," Pike said, "it'll take a helluva lot more than one shot to kill this one. You'd better get some rest. I want to start early in the morning."

121

"All right," Koloff said. He stared at the two women for a moment, then turned and went to his tent.

"Colonel!" Pike called out.

Makarov looked up. He was standing in front of the tent formerly shared by the three dead men. Pike assumed it was now his.

"You'll take first watch and I'll relieve you."

Makarov stared for a moment, then nodded.

"Charles!"

Severance had been sitting near his tent, holding his stomach and looking thoroughly miserable. At the sound of his name he looked up.

"You'll have to take a watch tonight. Are you up to it?"

Severance swallowed and then said, "Don't worry, I'll pull my weight."

"All right, then, get some rest and I'll wake you for your turn."

Severance nodded and went inside his tent.

"Vanya, can you spend the night out here with Sun Rising?"

"Of course," she said. "We will take care of your friend."

"Guess I lucked out, huh?" McConnell said. "I don't have to stand watch."

"Yeah," Pike said, looking at his friend with affection, "you lucky dog, you."

Chapter Fifteen

Halfway through his watch Pike felt the need for a cup of coffee. When he reached the fire he saw that McConnell was awake and sipping at a steaming cup himself.

"Can't sleep?" Pike asked.

"Who can sleep?" McConnell asked. "That monster came into camp, Pike, it came right after us. What do you think could have made it do that?"

Pike poured himself a cup of coffee and said, "I don't know, Skins."

"I know," Sun Rising said.

They had thought that both she and Vanya were asleep, but Sun Rising looked wide awake at the moment.

"You know what?" McConnell asked.

"Why the bear came into camp."

"Why?" Pike asked.

"Because it knows that you are after it."

McConnell frowned and asked, "Now how could it know that?"

"It knows," she said, "and it knows that it cannot be killed."

"That's nonsense," McConnell said. "All animals can be killed."

"Leonid hit it with his shot," Pike said, "I don't know

if I hit it with mine."

"If everyone hadn't been so panicked," McConnell said, "we might have gotten off more than one or two shots. We might have finished it right there and then."

"But we were panicked," Pike said, "all of us. Who could have expected that it would come into camp like that? It's . . . unbelievable."

"Wait until we tell this story," McConnell said. "They'll call us the biggest liars in the mountains."

"They will for sure," Pike said. "How are you feeling, partner?"

"I'm fine," McConnell said, but Pike noticed a glassiness to his eyes and a sheen of perspiration on his forehead.

"He has a fever," Pike said to Sun Rising.

"The wound is clean," she said. "He will be all right, but he must rest."

"You heard the lady, Skins," Pike said. "Lie down before I knock you down."

"All right," McConnell said. "I am feeling kind of sleepy."

Sun Rising helped him to lie down on his right side. He couldn't lie on his back because of the wound.

In minutes he was asleep.

"I'm going to take a turn around camp," Pike told Sun Rising.

Pike was sure—well, almost sure—that the bear wouldn't be back tonight. It had taken a few wounds and would want time to lick them. That would give them time to lick their wounds, as well.

Suddenly Pike and McConnell were not so outnumbered, but as a group they had lost much of their strength. A band of six or eight Crow or Blackfoot might figure them for easy prey now.

The smart thing to do would be to turn back and forget about the bear, but there were several reasons why they couldn't do that.

One, they were still being paid a lot of money to find it. After all the effort, and all that had happened, Pike wanted that money.

Two, the bear had taken a piece of McConnell with him. McConnell wanted his revenge, and so did Pike. When they were traveling together they were like one man. When someone took a piece of one of them, he took a piece of both.

Three, now that the bear had tasted their blood *it* might follow *them,* even if they turned back. They had to go on, find the beast, and destroy it.

If Sun Rising was right, if this was the bear that had killed some of her people, then it was already a man-killer.

Pike found some fresh bear tracks and checked the left hind paw. Sure enough, the little cut-out scar was there. At least it was comforting to know that there weren't *two* beasts this size roaming around.

Satisfied that the area was deserted, Pike went back to his post, a smooth stone he'd found to perch on, and proceeded to clean his Kentucky pistol. It had gotten wet when he dropped it in the snow during the attack. He kept his rifle within quick reach just in case.

When it came time to fetch Severance for his watch, Pike hesitated. He wasn't sure he wanted to place their lives in his hands. Maybe that was unfair. Even though he'd vomited twice, Severance had held up his end when they were burying the bodies. If he didn't wake the man for his watch, Severance might lose his self-confidence, and then he wouldn't be worth anything when they might really need him.

Pike wondered if the man could shoot at all. At the very least, they'd have to give him a gun to hold.

He went to Severance's tent and entered. He called the man's name twice before deciding to prod him. As soon as Pike touched him Severance leaped up, his eyes wide.

"Take it easy," Pike said, "it's only me."

125

"Pike," Severance said, as if he wasn't sure who Pike was.

"That's right," Pike said. "It's your watch."

For a moment he didn't think the man understood him, then Severance nodded, "Be right with you."

Pike stepped outside and in moments Severance joined him.

"You know how to use one of these?" Pike asked, holding his pistol out to the man.

"Sure I do," Severance said, accepting the weapon.

"All right," Pike said, "if you see or hear anything—or even *think* you see or hear anything—wake me up. Understand?"

"I understand."

"And if you have to fire that thing, make the shot count."

"Right."

"Are you up to this, Charles?"

Severance looked at Pike and said, "Yeah, I am. I want to do my part, Pike."

"All right, then," Pike said. "I'll turn in."

Severance was holding the pistol in two hands, one on the butt and the other around the barrel. He walked over to where Pike had been sitting and seated himself.

Pike went over to his blanket, which he had moved closer to McConnell. He went to sleep almost immediately. Once he awoke and saw Vanya sitting at the fire watching him. She didn't see his eyes open, and he closed them at once and drifted off to sleep again.

Pike woke later and realized that he had awakened because of Sun Rising. She was sitting near him and had been stroking his face. When she saw his eyes open she drew her hand back as quickly as if she had been burned.

"Sun Rising," he said. "Is everything all right?"

"Yes," she said, folding her hands in her lap. Her eyes were cast downward, as if she were embarrassed, and then she looked up at him.

"You were . . . moaning in your sleep," she said. "I sought to . . . comfort you. I am sorry I woke you. Please, go back to sleep."

Pike looked up. The beginnings of daylight were just starting to touch the sky. He propped himself up on an elbow and looked over at Severance. From what he could tell at this distance, the government man was still awake—and he was still holding the pistol in both hands. As he watched, Severance's head snapped up, as if he had heard something. His shoulders hunched as he listened, and then he relaxed, satisfied that he had heard nothing after all. Pike figured that most of Severance's watch had been spent this way. His shoulders would be sore by morning.

"What is it?" Sun Rising asked.

"Nothing," he replied. "Is that fresh coffee?"

She looked at the pot on the fire and said, "Yes. Would you like a cup?"

"Yes, please."

As she poured it he sat up and thought about what she had said. If indeed he had been moaning in his sleep he didn't remember what he had been moaning about. He wondered if he had been dreaming about a bear. He hoped not. He'd had enough of those kinds of dreams.

As Sun Rising handed him a steaming cup of coffee he asked, "How is McConnell?"

"He is resting easily," she said. "He will be fine."

"And you? How are you?"

"I am well."

"Are you getting enough rest?"

She smiled. "No, but neither is Vanya."

"I appreciate the both of you caring for him like this."

"It is important to keep him well," she said. "The bear will come back."

"Sun Rising," Pike said, "how much more do you know about this bear?"

"I have told you all I know," she said. "He will not die."

"I can't agree with that," he said. "There are enough of us to kill him if and when he comes back—or when we catch up to him."

"He will not run from you," she said. "He will lure you to your death."

"Our death?" he asked. "Are you including yourself in this?"

"If I am here," she said, "he will kill me, too."

Pike tried to remember what Sun Rising had been doing when the bear burst into the camp. He only remembered her stumbling out of the creature's way. Had it gone after her at all? That he couldn't remember.

"It will be daylight soon," Sun Rising said.

"Take Severance a cup of coffee, Sun Rising," Pike said. "He looks like he needs it."

"Yes."

As Sun Rising moved toward Severance, Vanya stirred and sat up. She stretched her arms over her head, thrusting her breasts out. Pike remembered what those breasts had felt like during that one time they had been together. He still did not know for sure if she had come to him on her own or if Koloff had sent her, but if he had to choose, he would say that she had come on her own.

Koloff did not strike him as the kind of man who would willingly share a woman—especially a woman as beautiful as Vanya.

"Good morning, Vanya."

Vanya finished stretching and then gave Pike a weary smile.

"I do not know how you do it," she said.

"Do what?"

"Sleep outside, on the ground," she said, "night after night."

128

"You get used to it. Coffee?"

"Yes, please."

He poured her a cup and handed it to her.

"What time is it?" she asked.

"It'll be light in half an hour. We'll get under way soon after."

"I will start breakfast," Sun Rising said, coming up behind them.

"No breakfast, Sun Rising," Pike said, "just coffee. The smell of food might bring the bear back before we're ready for him." He turned to Vanya and said, "Can you wake Koloff without angering him?"

"No," she said, standing, "but I will do it anyway."

"Good," Pike said, "tell him we've got to get going early if we want to catch up to his bear."

"All right."

"Say exactly that to him," Pike said, "tell him *his* bear."

"His bear," she said, nodding. "I will."

"I'll get Skins up."

"What if he is not able to travel?" Vanya asked.

"I don't know," Pike said. "We might have to leave him behind until he is able."

"You're not gonna leave me behind," McConnell said, sitting up. "I'll be ready to roll when you are."

Pike looked at Vanya and said, "Does that answer your question?"

While everyone else was breaking camp, stowing gear, and preparing to leave, Pike followed the tracks that the bear made when he charged through their camp. He found that after the bear had left the camp it had gone about twenty yards and then had circled around. In fact, he might even have circled the camp two or three times before finally going off in the direction he had come from. Was the animal actually considering another charge through the camp?

Before returning, Pike decided to wander over to where they had buried Koloff's men. As he approached, he noticed some splashes of red in the area, and more bear tracks . . . A coldness formed in the pit of his stomach as he approached the gravesite.

The snow was a deep red there, and the bodies had been dug up and further dismembered. They were hardly recognizable as human remains. If he hadn't known there were three of them, he would have been hard put to figure it out.

Pike decided that he would keep that little piece of information to himself.

"What did you find?" McConnell asked when he returned.

Koloff was nearby and came over before Pike could answer.

"Uh, nothing," Pike said.

"Nothing?" McConnell asked.

"You found nothing?" Koloff echoed.

McConnell realized that even if Pike had found something, he wasn't going to say so in front of the Russian.

"The bear apparently circled around the camp and then continued on in the direction we've been tracking it," Pike said. It was all he intended to say to Koloff. He'd tell McConnell about the rest when he got the chance to talk to him alone.

"So we simply have to keep moving in the direction we were going," Koloff said.

"That's right."

"Well then, shall we get under way?"

Pike looked at McConnell and said simply, "Let's."

Part Three
The Hunter Hunted

Chapter Sixteen

The general mood of the party had changed drastically. There was an apprehension and concentration in the group that had not been there before. Only Koloff and Makarov appeared unaffected by the tragedy that had befallen them.

Koloff seemed concerned only with bagging his bear. In fact, he was obsessed with the notion. Makarov, on the other hand, was as cold as ever—colder than a man could be—unless by force of sheer will. Nothing seemed to get to him in any way.

On her part, Sun Rising seemed serene, but to Pike's keen eye it appeared she knew more than she was saying.

"Skins, I'm going to drop back a bit," Pike told McConnell.

"Fine," McConnell said, looking down at the bear tracks they were following.

"You gonna be all right?"

McConnell looked at Pike only long enough to say, "I'm fine."

Pike slowed his horse and began to drop back.

"What is wrong?" Koloff asked when they were abreast.

"Nothing," Pike said. "I just want to ride behind for

133

a while."

"Will McConnell stay on the trail?"

"Are you kidding?" Pike asked. "He's a better tracker than I am."

Koloff looked doubtful, but Pike continued to drop behind until he was riding next to Sun Rising. He was on her left, while Vanya was on her right.

"Switch places with me," he said to Sun Rising.

"Why?"

"I want to talk to Vanya for a while."

Sun Rising frowned but maneuvered so that Pike was between her and Vanya. When Pike spoke to Vanya, his back was to Sun Rising.

"What is it?" Vanya asked.

"Tell me about Colonel Makarov."

"What do you want to know about him?"

"Whatever you know."

"That is not much."

"Just tell me."

She thought for a moment and said, "He is in love with me."

"You know that for a fact?"

"Yes."

"Is that why he came on this trip?"

"Oh, I am sure he came out of his loyalty to Ivan."

"Loyalty," Pike asked, "or love?"

"Love?" she said, laughing. "What makes you think he loves Ivan?"

"He seems very devoted—"

"He is devoted," she said, "and very serious about his job, which is keeping Ivan safe, but I do believe that when Ivan is finally killed by someone, it will be Colonel Makarov."

Pike stared at her for a moment then said, "Would you mind explaining that?"

"Makarov hates Ivan."

"Makarov—what's his first name?"

"Uri."

"If Uri hates Koloff, why did he take the job?"

"Ivan is important to Russia," Vanya said, "and Uri loves Russia."

"And you."

"And me."

"How do you feel about him?"

"He is Ivan's bodyguard."

"That's it?"

"There is nothing between Uri and me," she said, "if that is what you are worried about."

"I'm not worried."

"Good."

"If Makarov had to choose between you and Koloff, who would he choose?"

"There would not even be a choice."

"You?"

"Ivan."

"But you said he loves you."

"And Russia."

"He loves Russia more?"

"Yes."

"And Koloff is important to Russia."

"Yes," Vanya said. "You seem to have it all straight now."

"Do I?" Pike asked. "Then why do I feel so confused?"

"It is very simple," Vanya said. "As badly as Uri wants me, he will not shirk his duty."

"But you expect him to kill Koloff?"

She shrugged and said, "I am sure he will someday, but that day is not in the near future."

"I see."

"Is there anything else?"

"I take it that if you expect Uri to kill Ivan, it is because he is the better man?"

"Oh, yes," she said, "definitely. Ivan is a fine hunter,

the finest in Russia, but Uri is by far the better man."

"I see."

"It will be interesting to see who is the better man between you and Uri."

"And who would you bet on?"

"I would not bet," she said, "but I would watch with great interest."

"I bet you would," Pike said. He turned his head and saw Sun Rising watching him intently. He didn't know how much of the conversation she had been able to hear, but it really didn't matter.

Severance was riding behind them, so Pike dropped back even further to see how he was doing.

"How are you, Charles?"

"I never thought," Severance said, "that I would be in danger of falling asleep on horseback."

"I tell you what," Pike said, "I'll let you have the first watch so you can sleep the remainder of the night."

"That might work," Severance said. "Thank you."

"You did a fine job this morning."

"Did I?" the government man asked. "I was a little jumpy."

"That's perfect when you're on watch," Pike said. "It keeps you alert."

"Really?"

"Really," Pike said. "You're a natural."

"Thanks, Pike," Severance said. "Uh, can I ask you something?"

"Sure."

"I've been wondering about this ever since that beast invaded our camp last night."

"Wondering what?"

"You're the man with the experience, so maybe you could tell me."

"Tell you what?"

"Can that beast be killed?"

"Charles, of course it can be killed," Pike said. "Every living thing can die."

"But that . . . thing, that . . . apparition . . ." Severance's voice trailed off and he shuddered.

"Charles, it was a bear," Pike said. "Of course, it was a *large* bear, but it was just a bear."

Severance stared at him and said, "That was *just* a bear?"

Partly to allay his fears and partly to tease him and perhaps lighten his own spirits, Pike said, "Oh, sure. Wait until we run into a *really* big one."

Pike rode back up to join McConnell on the point, leaving behind a confused Severance, a pensive Vanya, and a puzzled Koloff, who was wondering what Pike had talked to the others about.

Koloff leaned over to Makarov and said, "Go and talk to Severance."

"About what?"

"Try to find out what he told Pike."

"Why do you think he would talk now?"

"He might have been so frightened last night that he is no longer afraid of us."

"I said earlier that we should have killed him."

"And I said I do not want to bring the entire American government down on us. Now go back and find out what he said. And make sure he is at least as frightened of us as he is of the bear."

Makarov nodded, wheeled his horse around roughly, and rode on back.

Makarov's rough handling of the horse alerted Pike to the fact that he was riding back to join Severance.

"What's wrong?" McConnell asked.

"Did you ever get the feeling that Severance was afraid of Koloff and Makarov?"

"Severance? He's afraid of everything."

"Yeah, but . . ." Pike said, looking over his shoulder. Makarov was riding alongside Severance, doing all the

137

talking.

"But what?"

Pike looked at McConnell again and said, "I can't help feeling there are things going on here that we don't know anything about."

"What did you find out from Vanya?"

"Not much that helps," Pike said. "Apparently Makarov loves her and hates Koloff, but he loves Russia more than anything. If it came down to a choice he'd pick Koloff over Vanya, because Koloff is important to Russia. Hey, I think I got it right!"

"If you say so," McConnell said.

Chapter Seventeen

They chose not to take a break in the afternoon, and instead rode straight through to early evening.

They were about an hour away from stopping for the night when Pike called a halt.

"We're not making camp yet, are we?" Koloff called out, his tone annoyed. "We have plenty of light."

Pike turned in his saddle and called back, "We're not stopping, but I want everyone to wait here while Skins and I ride ahead."

"Why?" Koloff asked.

"Yeah, why?" McConnell chimed in.

"I don't know," Pike said, looking at his partner. "For the past hour I've had the feeling we're being watched."

"By Indians? Or by a bear?"

"I don't know."

McConnell kept his head still, but flicked his eyes about to take a look.

"Pike, it can't be a bear watching us," he said in a low voice. "That ain't natural."

"I know."

"Why are we waiting?" Koloff called out.

Pike looked straight ahead. The ground was remarkably flat, an open area covered with white snow. On either side there were high slopes, and behind any of them could have been a small band of Indians . . . or a large bear. If they were caught out in the open, with no cover . . .

Pike turned his horse to face Koloff.

"McConnell and I are going to ride ahead and make sure it's safe."

"What makes you think it is not safe?" Koloff asked.

"There's too much open ground," Pike said. "I don't want to risk having us all caught out in the open. Just stay here and wait until we signal you to come."

Koloff looked annoyed, but agreed.

They started their horses, moving at a slow and easy pace out into the clearing.

"It's quiet," Pike said.

"Too quiet," McConnell agreed.

"Something . . ."

Suddenly, there was a loud noise—a roar!

"There!" Pike shouted.

Over the top of a slope came the bear. The creature moved with incredible speed, charging right at them.

"Jesus," McConnell said.

For a moment both men were frozen, rooted to the spot, as were their horses. The poor frightened animals didn't know which way to run.

"Split up!" Pike shouted. "Now! We'll confuse it!"

They split up, riding away from each other. The bear reached the spot where they had been sitting and wheeled about in a circle . . . once, twice, confused . . .

Koloff shouted as the bear charged.

"There it is!"

Makarov grabbed his rifle.

"No one is to shoot!" Koloff shouted, grabbing his own rifle. "He is mine!"

He kicked his horse's ribs and started toward the animal, which he knew would not stay confused for long.

Eventually the bear would decide which man to chase . . .

Pike and McConnell rode away from each other, then both wheeled around and jammed their rifle butts to their shoulders.

"No!" Koloff shouted. "Do not fire!"

Both men hesitated, but then Pike fired anyway. His ball struck the bear just below its right shoulder. The animal roared as its blood stained the snow. Then it stood up on its hind legs.

McConnell fired, striking the bear dead center. The animal bellowed in pain and came down onto all fours again.

Koloff kept riding as the wounded animal tried to decide where to run. Pike and McConnell were hurriedly reloading.

Koloff was grinning as he gripped his saddle with both knees and released his horse's reins so that he could aim his rifle. What he did not anticipate was that the horse, smelling the bear, would refuse to approach. The horse balked, shying away. Koloff tried to lead the horse with the pressure of his knees, but instead the horse reared, dumping him unceremoniously in the snow, and then ran off . . .

The bear, spying the man on the ground, chose him as the easiest prey and charged . . .

Seeing Koloff fall, Makarov kicked his horse into action, taking up his rifle . . .

Pike instantly realized the danger Koloff was in and abandoned the attempt to load his rifle. He dropped it into the snow, took up his Kentucky pistol, and rode to-

141

ward the fallen Koloff . . .

McConnell decided to drop down off his horse so that he'd be able to reload. He wanted to be ready to fire if Pike and Makarov could not rescue Koloff . . .

Koloff quickly got to his feet, his hands empty. He looked around, saw his rifle on the ground, and picked it up, hoping it would still fire. Then he turned and saw the bear running at him. Beyond the bear he saw Pike riding up, his pistol in his hand. Suddenly, he heard a shot from behind and shouted, "No!"

Makarov fired, his ball striking the bear near its left shoulder. Far from a killing shot. He reversed his grip on the rifle to use it as a club if he had to, and continued on toward the immense beast.

Pike was still too far away to fire, but his horse was moving faster than the bear. He might, just might, get close enough before the bear reached Koloff . . . He had to admire the Russian's coolness. Koloff was standing his ground, ready to fire when the bear got close enough . . .

Makarov reached Koloff before the bear did and sprang down from his horse. He stood next to the man he was sworn to protect, holding the rifle by the barrel.

"Get behind me!" he told Koloff.

"Nonsense!" Koloff shouted. "When he is close enough I will fire. Stand aside!"

Koloff noticed that Pike was catching up to the bear

and pointing his pistol dead at him. From that angle Pike would not have a killing shot, so Koloff did not bother to shout. He would stand his ground. When the bear reached him it would stand up on its hind legs, and then Koloff would have the killing shot.

He had only to wait . . .

Pike knew that the bear had been hit at least three times. He could only fire into the bear's back, a shot he doubted would kill it, but he had to try. The bear was almost on top of Koloff.

Pike pointed the pistol at the bear, feeling as if he were riding down a buffalo, and fired . . .

Koloff saw Pike fire, but the animal never slowed.

Good.

"Ivan—" Makarov shouted.

"Stand aside, Uri!" Koloff roared. "This is my bear."

Pike had fired. There was nothing he could do now but watch . . .

Makarov moved away from Koloff, looking on helplessly as the man he was sworn to protect stood alone in the path of a charging bear . . .

McConnell got down on one knee, sighted down the barrel of his rifle, and waited . . .

Koloff was alone. As far as he was concerned, there was only himself and the bear in the whole world.

Only one thing could go wrong, and that was if the bear continued its charge and did not stop to rear up on its hind legs.

Koloff chose to believe that the animal would stop, and stood fast.

As the bear closed the distance it suddenly slowed. It was almost on him when it finally stopped and rose on its hind legs, bleeding from four wounds.

In a flash Koloff realized that he wasn't sure where the bear's heart was. He aimed at the animal's massive throat, beneath its slobbering jaw, and fired . . .

Chapter Eighteen

They congregated around the dead bear.

"I said no one was to fire," Koloff said loudly.

"You had the killing shot, Koloff," Pike said.

"Yes," Koloff said, "so I did."

Pike looked up at the sky.

"We'd better camp. We'll go on a little further and pitch a camp."

"I want the skin," Koloff said.

"Tomorrow," Pike insisted, "when it's light."

"I want it tonight."

"The bear's not going anywhere, Koloff," Pike said sharply.

Koloff looked down at the bear and said, "No, it is not."

"Skins, take them further on and find someplace to camp."

"Let's go, people."

Pike walked over and stood next to Sun Rising, who was staring down at the bear.

"You see?" he said. "It's dead."

She looked up at him and then back down at the dead bear.

"Come on, Sun Rising," Pike said. "Let's make camp. I'm sure that after this everyone is hungry."

She walked to her horse and mounted up, following the others.

Pike leaned over the bear and tried to count the wounds. The bear was lying on its left side, and he knew there was one wound there. There was one on the right shoulder and one in the back, both fired by Pike. There was the shot by Makarov, and then the killing shot fired by Koloff.

Or was it the killing shot?

There was a sixth wound, in the side of the bear's neck. Pike remembered McConnell down on one knee, preparing to fire if the need arose.

Had he fired? He must have, because there was one extra wound on the bear, one that indeed could have been the killing shot.

Even if McConnell had fired, maybe they'd just keep that little fact to themselves, he told himself. Now that Koloff had his bear, the game was over and they could get on with their lives.

All of them.

The camp was quiet. Koloff and Makarov were in their tent with Vanya. Sun Rising was cooking. Leonid was watching Sun Rising cook. Severance was inside his tent, doing whatever it was he did when he was there.

Pike and McConnell were sitting at the fire with Sun Rising.

"What's wrong?" McConnell asked.

Pike looked at Leonid, who did not seem to be paying attention.

"He's all right," McConnell said. "What is it?"

"Something's been bothering me ever since the other night, when the bear came into camp."

"What?"

"Well, I never had a chance to tell you, but the next morning I found the three bodies. They had been dug up

146

and torn apart."

"Jesus."

"That's not all," Pike said. "I just realized what's been bothering me."

"What?"

"The tracks around the bodies."

"What about them?"

"They were different."

"You mean . . ."

Pike nodded.

"They weren't made by the same bear."

"You mean there's two of them?"

Pike nodded.

"How do you like that?" McConnell said.

"There's more."

"What? More?"

Pike nodded again.

"The bear we killed—that *you* killed with a shot that was not to be believed—"

"Flatterer."

"—was not the same bear that attacked our camp. It's not the same bear we've been tracking."

"Wait a minute," McConnell said, "how many bears are we talking about?"

"Two," Pike said, "maybe mates, a male and a female. That dead one is a female and it doesn't have that scar on its paw—you know, that mark in the tracks we've been following?"

"So you're saying that the male attacked our camp and killed three men, but the female dug up the bodies and . . . fed on them?"

"Right."

"And because the bear had tasted human meat, she attacked us today?"

"Right again."

"Then the mate is still out there—the original bear?"

"The bigger one, Skins," Pike said. "This one was

147

smaller than the one that attacked the camp."

"Are you sure?"

"I am."

McConnell frowned.

"You know, I thought that when we first saw him, but I wasn't sure."

"Well, be sure. There's another bear out there."

"So? What do we do now? Tell Koloff?"

"If we do he's going to want to go on."

"And we want to get this over with and get away from him."

"Right."

Sun Rising came over and handed them each a plate of food.

"I told you," she said, looking at Pike, "the bear could not be killed."

"You knew this wasn't the same bear, didn't you?" Pike asked.

"Yes."

"Why didn't you tell us?"

She shrugged.

"You knew also," she said, and went back to the fire to prepare more plates.

Pike looked at McConnell and said, "What do you think, partner?"

McConnell reached up and touched his wounded shoulder.

"The one that got me is still out there?"

"Right."

McConnell lowered his hand.

"I say let's go after him."

"Vengeance?"

"Damn right."

"All right, then," Pike said. "We'll tell Koloff — after dinner."

* * *

When they had finished eating and had turned the plates over to Sun Rising, Pike said, "I'll go and tell him."

"I'll leave that to you."

"Thanks."

Pike walked to Koloff's tent and reached it just as Makarov stuck his head out.

"Oh," Pike said. "I want to talk to him."

"He wants to talk to you," Makarov said, backing away to allow Pike to enter.

Inside Pike saw Vanya sitting at one end of the tent and Koloff at the other. He had the feeling that there had been an argument. He could feel the tension in the air.

"Ah, Pike," Koloff said. "I wanted to talk to you."

"And I to you," Pike said.

Pike felt the barrel of a gun poke him in the ribs and turned his head. Makarov was holding his rifle and staring at Pike.

"What the—" Pike said.

"Perhaps I'd better talk first," Koloff said. "Uri, get his pistol."

Makarov slid Pike's pistol from his belt.

"What the hell is going on?" Pike demanded.

"The bear is vanquished," Koloff said. "It is time to go on to the next challenge."

"And what is that?" Pike asked.

"You will find out very soon," Koloff said. He put his hand out and Makarov tossed him Pike's Kentucky pistol.

"Go outside and get McConnell's gun," Koloff ordered. "I will hold Pike here until you do."

Makarov nodded and went outside.

Pike turned around and looked at Vanya.

"I did not—" she started, but Koloff cut her off.

"Go outside, Vanya. I will call for you later."

Vanya stood up, gave Pike a pleading look, and then

149

left the tent.

"What's going on, Ivan?" Pike asked.

Koloff stood up and faced Pike, the Kentucky pistol pointing at the bigger man.

"You have repeatedly sought to embarrass me in front of my people, Pike."

"I have not," Pike said. "I've been doing what I think is right."

"You want Vanya and you want Sun Rising and you want to show them that you are the better man. Well, I am going to give you that chance."

"I repeat," Pike said. "What the hell are you talking about?"

"Uri should have your friend's gun by now. Let us go outside."

Pike hesitated a moment, then turned and went outside. Koloff followed, but not too closely. He had seen Pike move and knew how deceptively fast he was for a big man.

Outside Pike saw Makarov standing by the fire covering McConnell. There were confused looks on the faces of Leonid and Sun Rising. Vanya was standing off to one side, hugging her arms and looking away. To her credit, she seemed miserable over the turn of events.

Still, Pike didn't really know what this turn of events meant, and he clearly wasn't going to be able to rush Koloff into telling them.

"Get over there by your friend," Koloff told Pike.

Pike obeyed, walking over and standing next to McConnell.

"What's going on?" McConnell asked him.

"I'm afraid we're going to have to wait for him to tell us that."

Koloff said something to Leonid, who hesitated and then went into his tent and came out with some rope. He got behind Pike and McConnell and tied their hands behind their backs.

"I am sorry," he said, before tightening the ropes on McConnell's wrists and moving away.

"There something ironic about this," Pike said, and McConnell knew what he meant. The first time the Russians had laid eyes on them they were tied with their hands behind their backs.

"All right, Ivan," Pike said, "now that we're trussed up suppose you tell us what this is all about."

Ivan Koloff came over and stood directly in front of Pike.

"It is about you and me, Pike," Koloff said. "You and I are going to have another contest to see who is the better man."

Pike frowned and asked, "What kind of contest?"

"A simple kind," Koloff said. "The contest of the hunter and the hunted. I will be the hunter." With a laugh Koloff asked, "Can you guess who the hunted will be?"

Pike looked at McConnell, who stared back.

"You want to guess?"

"I have a pretty good idea who the hunted will be," McConnell said, "but maybe I'm wrong."

"I don't think so," Pike said. He looked at Koloff's smiling face and said, "I think we both have a pretty good idea who it will be."

"Good," Koloff said, smiling, "good, you keep your humor. That is good. Perhaps you will need it."

"Tell me something, Ivan," Pike said.

"If I can."

"Will you be hunting one or both of us?"

"I have given that a great deal of thought, Pike," Koloff said.

"You feel like sharing your thoughts with us?" McConnell asked.

"Of course. I have observed how close the two of you are. It is my opinion that if I kill Pike I shall have to kill McConnell soon thereafter, simply to keep him from coming after me. Am I correct?"

"As right as you can be," McConnell said.

"So, for that reason I believe that I shall hunt down and kill you both."

"That makes you a little outnumbered, doesn't it?" Pike asked.

"Well, there is, of course, the fact that I will be armed and you will not," Koloff said. "And to even it out, Colonel Makarov will be joining my little hunt. So in effect, it will be the two of you against the two of us."

McConnell looked at Pike and asked, "Which one do you want?"

"Oh," Pike said, "I think I'll take the little one."

McConnell frowned and asked, "Which one is the little one?"

"As far as I'm concerned," Pike said, "both of them."

Chapter Nineteen

Pike and McConnell were put in Severance's tent. They were surprised to find that Severance was imprisoned with them.

"They have to kill me sooner or later," Severance told them.

"Why?"

"They can't allow me to get back to Washington alive. Not knowing what I know."

Pike leaned forward and said, "Tell me, Charles, what do you know?"

"Yeah," McConnell added, "what we should have known before?"

"Koloff and Makarov, they've killed before."

"What do you mean?" McConnell asked. "You mean, in the war or something?"

"No," Severance said, "on this trip. You see, when Koloff gets tired of hunting animals he hunts people."

"And you kept this to yourself?"

Severance looked away and said, "I was afraid—I *am* afraid, gentlemen. I have known for a long time that I am a coward."

"Nobody is a coward, Charles," Pike said. "You just have to find the right situation to bring out your courage."

"I'm afraid I have no courage to bring out," Severance said.

"I think I agree with him, Pike," McConnell said.

"Well, I don't," Pike said, "but let's not talk about that now."

"Why not?" McConnell asked. "What else have we got to talk about?"

"Surviving. Koloff intends to put us out there on foot, with no food and no weapons. We've survived for days under those conditions before, but not with armed men hunting us down."

"What do you suggest?"

"We'll have to come up with some sort of a plan," Pike said. "When he lets us go, we have to know where we're going and what we're going to do."

"Okay," McConnell said, "you tell me, what *are* we going to do?"

Pike hesitated, then said, "I don't know. I haven't figured that out yet."

"You cannot do this," Vanya said.

"Why not?" Koloff asked. "We've done it before."

"We are not in our own country, Ivan," Vanya said. "You are taking chances with our lives."

"That is called living, Vanya," Koloff said. "One is not alive unless he takes chances with his life—or with hers."

"I do not want to take chances with mine," she said, sitting up.

They were lying down in Koloff's tent. He had pulled her down with him and roughly removed her clothes, after which they'd had sex. It was as close to being rape as it could be without actually being so.

Now he reached over and cupped her left breast. He stroked it as he spoke.

"Vanya, you must decide who you are with, Pike or

154

me. I know that you have been with him and I know that you want him again, but he is a dead man."

"Perhaps not," she said. "Even after you release him you still have to find him and kill him."

His fingers found her nipple and twisted it cruelly.

"And you think that I will not?"

"He is not like the others you have hunted," she said, wincing from the pain.

"I know he is not," he agreed. "That is what will make this hunt all the more satisfying."

He pressed his hands against her chest now and pushed her back down. Thinking about the hunt had gotten him hard again. He spread her legs roughly and drove himself into her. She cried out in pain. He pinned her wrists above her head and drove himself into her as hard and deep as he could, and kept driving until he emptied into her, bellowing out loud.

When Koloff was done with her he pulled her to her feet and pushed her away from him.

"Get dressed and get me Sun Rising."

"I am not enough for you anymore?" she asked, her tone mocking.

"Just get her, and do not talk back to me, Vanya. I am not in the mood."

She dressed herself and was in such a hurry to get out of the tent that she stumbled through the flap.

Makarov saw Vanya stumble from Koloff's tent and knew that Koloff had taken and dismissed her. He didn't like it when Koloff treated Vanya badly. If not for his love of his motherland, Ivan Koloff would not see another sunrise.

* * *

155

Vanya went to the fire, where Sun Rising was sitting. The Crow squaw was pouring coffee into some cups.

"He wants you," Vanya said.

Sun Rising looked up at Vanya with sympathy.

"He will do to me what he has done to you?"

"Yes," Vanya said. "I am sorry, Sun Rising. Just do not get him angry and he will not hurt you."

Sun Rising stood up and faced Vanya.

"I was pouring coffee for Pike and the others."

"I will take it to them."

Sun Rising started away, then turned back.

"If I fight him, will he kill me?"

"In his present frame of mind, yes," Vanya said.

"I must stay alive," Sun Rising said, "to help Pike."

"Then let him do what he wants," Vanya said. "When he is done he will let you go. He likes to sleep alone the night before a manhunt."

Sun Rising nodded and started for Koloff's tent.

Vanya finished pouring the coffee and carried it to the tent where Pike and the others were being held. Leonid was on guard.

"Coffee for them," Vanya said.

Leonid looked past her toward Koloff's tent, then said, "All right. Bring it."

Vanya knew that Leonid was no happier than she was with what was going on. He liked McConnell and Pike. She also knew he would never stand against Koloff.

She had often thought that she would never stand against him either.

But perhaps that had changed.

Pike looked up as Vanya entered. Her hair was disheveled and she looked as if she had dressed hurriedly. He knew what must have happened.

"I have coffee for you," she said.

Pike and McConnell's hands were tied. Severance's

hands were not.

"We can't drink it with our hands tied."

"He will have to hold the cups for you," she said, nodding at Severance. "I cannot untie you."

"All right," Pike said.

She put the cups down next to them.

"Are you all right?" Pike asked.

"Yes."

"Has he hurt you?"

"He will not hurt me."

"And Sun Rising?"

She hesitated and then said, "He will not hurt her either."

She stood up to leave, then turned back.

"Pike, I did not know—"

"You knew that he had hunted other men?"

"Yes."

"Then you could have guessed what he was going to do to us."

"Yes," she said, lowering her eyes.

Pike didn't say anything else and Vanya left. When she was gone he looked at Severance.

"Let's get some of that coffee into us," Pike said.

While Koloff invaded her body Sun Rising simply lay still, not moving. Koloff slid his hands beneath her, cupping her buttocks, and grunted with effort as he took her in long, hard strokes. Sun Rising stared at the top of the tent and pretended that it was a blue sky— an endless blue sky.

"You like it," Koloff grunted in her ear. "You want it . . ."

She did not say a word.

"Go," Koloff told her later. "You are useless. You

157

have no feelings. Is that the way all Crow women are?"

She dressed and didn't answer.

"Get out!" he shouted. "In the morning you're going to skin that bear for me. Understand?"

"I understand."

"Now get out."

Sun Rising joined Vanya at the fire.

"Are you all right?" Vanya asked.

"Yes."

"We have to do something to save Pike."

"Yes."

"But what?"

Sun Rising looked at Vanya and began to speak . . .

Pike was watching McConnell when his friend started to doze off.

"Go ahead," Pike said, "go to sleep. We're going to need all the rest we can get."

"What about you?"

"I've always been the brains of this duo," Pike said. "I'll stay awake and think of something."

"Brains . . ." McConnell mused. "If I wasn't so tired I'd argue with you . . ."

"Would you like me to stand watch?" Severance asked Pike.

Pike looked at the man and then said, not without some irony, "Sure, Charles, stand watch."

Chapter Twenty

When Pike opened his eyes the next morning he saw Charles Severance watching the flap of the tent intently. He turned his head and saw that McConnell was still sleeping. He had to move to remind himself that his hands were tied. He'd forgotten because he could no longer *feel* his hands.

There was a shaft of light coming in through the flap so he knew it was morning.

"How long has it been light?" he asked Severance.

Severance jumped at the sound of Pike's voice.

"About fifteen minutes."

McConnell opened his eyes and said, "Well, brains, have you come up with anything?"

"We're too far from any settlement to walk it," Pike said, "even if we survive until dark."

"We can survive until dark," McConnell said, "but what about after dark? We can't survive overnight without some blankets and a fire."

"A fire will be easy enough," Pike said. "We'll just have to make sure it's hidden. We have nothing to cook, so we won't have to worry about them following the scent."

"What do you mean, we have nothing to cook? We can catch something."

"The smell of cooking meat would give our position away," Pike said. "Besides, we're not going to have time to eat."

"Why not?"

Pike was about to answer and then thought better of it. Severance certainly wouldn't volunteer anything they said to Koloff, but the Russian was sure to question him, and the less he had to say, the better.

"We'll talk about it later," Pike said.

Severance didn't seem to realize that it was his presence that was keeping them from discussing their plans now.

"Do you really think you can survive out there until dark?" he asked. "With no weapons, no water, no—"

"There's plenty of water, Charles," Pike said, "and weapons can be made. Koloff is putting us out on foot in our own element. He knows we can catch or make whatever we might need."

"Then why is he doing it?" Severance asked, looking puzzled.

"Because in his arrogance he doesn't think it will make a difference. He and Makarov will be armed with rifles, and they'll be on horseback. They think that gives them an insurmountable advantage."

"Doesn't it?" Severance asked.

Yeah," McConnell said, "doesn't it?"

Pike looked at McConnell and said, "It's an *almost* insurmountable advantage."

"Well, I'm glad to hear that," McConnell said. "For a minute there I thought we were in *real* trouble."

Pike was about to say something else when the tent flap was thrown back and Leonid entered.

"He wants you outside," he said.

Pike made to get up and then fell back.

"Can we get our hands untied?"

160

"Not yet," Leonid said. "I will help you up."

Leonid and Severance got Pike and McConnell to their feet.

"I hope he's going to let us have some breakfast before he lets us go," McConnell said.

Leonid had nothing to say to that.

"On the other hand," McConnell said, "who wants to run around on a full stomach?"

Outside they squinted at the glare of the sun reflecting off the white snow.

"Bring them here!" Koloff shouted.

He was standing by the fire with Makarov. Sun Rising and Vanya stood off to the side, looking on helplessly.

As Pike and McConnell approached Koloff looked at Sun Rising and said, "What are you waiting for? Go and skin my bear."

Sun Rising caught Pike's eyes and Pike thought she was trying to tell him something. Then he noticed that the knife in her hand was his. She was going to use his knife to skin the bear.

"And take Vanya with you," Koloff said. "Teach her how to do it."

Vanya looked at Pike, but there was only helplessness in her eyes.

What was it that Sun Rising was trying to tell him?

"The hunt begins now, gentlemen," Koloff said. He nodded, and Leonid slit the ropes that were holding Pike and McConnell's hands. Almost immediately fiery little needles began to course through Pike's hands as the blood began to circulate. He and McConnell tried to rub life back into them.

"You have an hour's head start," Koloff said.

"That's very sporting of you," Pike said.

"That is what this is, Pike," Koloff said. "Sport."

161

"To you, maybe."

"Come now," Koloff said, "you can't tell me you are not looking forward to this opportunity to show that you are truly the better man."

"I don't need to go through this to find that out," McConnell said. "I already know he's the better man."

As if propelled by some unspoken order from Koloff, Makarov stepped forward and hit McConnell in the stomach with his fist. McConnell started to double over but stopped himself. He did not want to give the Russian the satisfaction.

"You had both better get moving," Koloff said. "The hour has begun."

"Come on," Pike said, grabbing McConnell's arm.

"What about me?" Severance asked.

Jesus, Pike thought, don't send him with us. He'll just slow us down.

"Do you want to go with them, Charles?" Koloff asked. "Out there?"

Severance looked at Pike and McConnell, then looked away in shame.

"No," he said, "I want to stay here."

"With me?"

"Yes," Severance said, "with you."

"Good," Koloff said. "You can stay—in fact, you can make breakfast, since my other squaw is busy."

Pike felt sorry for Severance, but he quickly shook it off. He didn't have time for that.

He and McConnell turned and started walking away from camp.

"Run!" Koloff shouted. "You only have an hour."

They walked, conserving their energy. It was also meant as a small gesture of saving face. They did not want the Russians to see them running away from the camp.

162

Like it makes a real difference, Pike thought, whether we walk or run.

When they had put some distance between themselves and the camp they stopped.

"I wasn't sure we were going to get out of there," McConnell confided. "I kept expecting to get a bullet in the back."

"Not from Koloff," Pike said. "He's serious about this. He wants to prove he's the better man."

"Seems to me that's generally proved on more equal terms."

"We'll just have to make due with the terms we have," Pike said, looking around. "Let's not forget that other bear is out here someplace, minus a mate."

"That's right," McConnell said. "We just plumb forgot to tell Makarov about that. Maybe the bear will get them before they get us."

"That would be nice," Pike said, "but on foot we make much easier prey for the bear than they do. Let's just keep our eye out for him."

"Where are we headed?" McConnell asked. "Now that we're out of camp and away from Severance, you can tell me."

"We're not headed anywhere."

"What?"

"We're just going to circle around some, try and stay ahead of them until nightfall."

"And then?"

"And then we're going back into camp. We've got to take the offensive, Skins. If we stay on the defensive we haven't got a chance."

"So how do you propose to stay ahead of them?"

"We're going to have to lay false trails, double back,

and just generally do what we can to confuse them."

"We could split up," McConnell said, "and meet later. Maybe they'll split up too. We might even get a chance to jump them."

"We might, but my gut feeling is that Koloff is too smart for that. Let's stay together a while and see what happens."

"All right," McConnell said, "you're calling the shots, but only because you had all night to think up this very impressive plan."

"Are you kidding?" Pike asked. "I fell asleep right after you did."

"Now that," McConnell said, "is real comforting."

Chapter Twenty-one

Vanya watched with distaste as Sun Rising skinned the bear, cleanly removing the coat from the carcass.

"Ivan will treasure this bear coat," Vanya said.

"I would poison it if I could," Sun Rising said.

"Poison it?"

"Coat the inside with poison so that when he wears it the poison would eat into his flesh."

"You could do that?"

"If I had the poison," Sun Rising said, "which I do not."

When Sun Rising was finished she turned the bear-skin inside out so that the sun would dry the inside.

"Won't they come looking for us?" Vanya asked.

"Who?" Sun Rising asked. "Koloff and Mak . . . Mak . . .the silent one are hunting for Pike and Mc-Connell." Sun Rising had a problem with Makarov's name. "The other . . ."

"Leonid?"

"Yes," she said. "Would he come looking for us?"

"No."

"Then we can sit here in the sun waiting for the coat to dry."

That said, Sun Rising took Pike's knife—the knife she had used to skin the bear—and pushed it into the cut she had made down the bear's middle.

"What are you doing?" Vanya asked.

"I am leaving the knife there for Pike."

"Pike? But how will he know it is there?"

"He will know," Sun Rising said. "He will find it."

"But this is so open," Vanya said. "He can't just walk up to the bear and take the knife out. He would be out in the open."

"He will come after dark."

"If he is alive when darkness comes."

"He will be."

"How can you be so sure?"

"Pike is He-Whose-Head-Touches-the-Sky," Sun Rising said. "He cannot die."

"That is what you said about the bear."

"The bear did not die."

"How can you say that? You just skinned it."

"This is not the bear that attacked our camp."

"What?"

"This bear is smaller," Sun Rising said, "and she was a female. She is the mate of the one who attacked us."

"You mean . . . that monster is still out here somewhere?"

"Yes."

"Does Pike know?"

"Yes."

"And Ivan?"

Sun Rising almost smiled as she said, "No."

"Look," McConnell said.

Pike had already seen it.

Bear tracks.

"There's the mark," Pike said, pointing to the left hind track.

166

"That's him, all right," McConnell said, "and he's near."

"Let's double back here and leave a second set of tracks," Pike suggested.

"You want to lead Koloff away from these bear tracks?" McConnell asked.

"Yes," Pike replied. "The longer he goes without realizing there's another bear out here, the better it might be for us."

"Because there's more of a chance they'll go walking right into each other."

"Right."

"Maybe they'll kill each other and make it easy on us," McConnell suggested.

"When has it ever been easy on us up here, Skins?" Pike asked.

"Never."

"That's why we love it so much."

"Yeah," McConnell said. "We're a couple of crazy men, all right."

Pike took a deep breath, filling his lungs with cold Rocky Mountain air, and said, "I wouldn't have it any other way."

"You really think we're going to come out of this, don't you?"

"Yup."

"Why?"

"Because Koloff is too arrogant, too cocky," Pike said. "He's going to make a mistake, not us."

"I wish I was as sure as you are."

"I'm sure enough for the both of us," Pike lied. He was sure, but not that sure.

Not yet.

Koloff looked down at the tracks and smiled.

"What is it?" Makarov asked.

"A false trail."

"How can you be sure?"

"I know Pike," Koloff said. "I have been studying him. I know how he thinks and I know what he will do."

"Then which way do we go?"

"We go this way," Koloff said, turning his horse.

"Will we catch them before nightfall?" Makarov asked.

"I doubt it," Koloff said. "Pike is at home out here."

"Then it was foolish to let him and McConnell go," Makarov said.

"Not foolish, my friend," Koloff said. "Daring."

The two words meant the same to Makarov.

"After dark he will try to come back into camp," Koloff said, "and we will be waiting for him."

"Then why are we out here?"

"For the air, Uri," Koloff said. "Smell it. Fill your lungs with it. There is no sweeter air on earth."

"Air . . ." Makarov muttered. As far as he was concerned, they should have killed both Pike and McConnell a long time ago. Hell, they should have let the *Indians* kill them.

Severance sat on one side of the fire, Leonid on the other. There was a rifle near Leonid. For a few moments Severance entertained the idea of trying to get the rifle, but he immediately abandoned it. He was not a hero; he knew that.

"Do you approve of what Koloff is doing?" he asked Leonid.

"It is not for me to approve or disapprove," Leonid

said.

"But . . . you like McConnell, don't you? And Pike?"

"That does not matter."

"But you do?"

Grudgingly Leonid said, "Yes."

"So do I. Maybe together there is something we can do for them."

Leonid stared at Severance coldly and then looked away. The man's expression told Severance that if he was ever going to join forces with anyone, it would not be with him.

Not that Severance could blame him.

As the day wore on Sun Rising and Vanya held their place, as did Leonid and Severance.

Pike and McConnell were not experiencing any particular hardship. They had been afoot on this terrain many times, some of those times without weapons or food. There would not be any problem until night—and the temperature—fell.

Koloff looked up at the sky.

"It is time to go back to camp," he announced.

As far as Makarov was concerned, it was long past that time. Instead, he said, "There is still some light left."

"I knew we would not find them out here," Koloff remarked. "They know the terrain too well. We will wait for them back at camp."

"What if they do not come back to camp?"

"They will," Koloff said. "They've nowhere else to go. They'll come back."

* * *

169

"Time for us to go back," Sun Rising said, looking at the sky.

That was fine with Vanya. It was already starting to get cold.

"Cold?" Sun Rising asked.

"Yes."

"We can wrap this around us if you like." Sun Rising said, indicating the bearskin.

The inside of the skin was still too fresh for Vanya's taste, so she said, "That's all right."

"Help me carry it, then."

Vanya hefted part of the heavy skin, and they started back to camp.

"Something just occurred to me," Pike said.

"What?"

They were both sitting on a rock, taking a little rest. McConnell was hefting a sliver of stone he'd found. It had a point, but he wished there were some way he could sharpen the sides.

"Koloff knows that he'll never find us out here. We know our way around too well."

"Then why let us go? We could get away."

"And go where?"

McConnell shrugged and said, "I don't know."

"He knows we have to return to the camp."

"So why chase us around out here?"

Pike shrugged and said, "Maybe for the exercise. Besides, I'm sure he's gone back to camp by now."

"And he's waiting for us."

"Right."

"And we don't have any choice but to go back anyway, right?"

"Right again."

"Unarmed."

"You have a weapon."

"You call this a weapon?" McConnell asked, holding up his stone dagger.

Suddenly Pike smiled. "I think I know where to find a real knife."

"Where?"

"Come on," Pike said, getting up, "I'll show you."

"It's been skinned," McConnell said.

"I can see that."

"Why did we come here?"

Lying on their bellies on a rise, they could see the freshly-skinned bear in the clearing below them.

"Before we left camp Sun Rising was trying to tell me something."

"I didn't hear her say a thing."

"She was trying to convey something to me with her eyes."

"With her eyes? You could read her eyes?"

"I think I could," Pike said. "She was carrying my knife and she was on her way out here to skin the dead bear. What does that suggest to you?"

"That she was going to use your knife to skin the bear."

"You're quick, Skins."

"Come on, Pike," McConnell said, "I never learned how to read a Crow squaw's eyes."

"I think she hid the knife."

"Where?"

"Either near the bear or under it . . . or even inside it."

"Your knife? You think it's out there?"

"I hope so."

"How do you suggest we get it? Walk right out there and stuff our hands into the innards of a bear?"

"Exactly that," Pike said, "only we'll wait until after dark to do it."

"It's pretty near dark now," McConnell said, "and I ain't got nothing better to do. I sure hope you're reading that squaw's eyes right."

"So do I."

Neither man knew that at that very moment there was another set of eyes looking down at the carcass. Eyes burning with hatred even while a bestial heart longed for its mate.

Chapter Twenty-two

When it was as dark as it was ever going to get McConnell said, "Well, if we're going down there, we might as well do it now.

They had started down to the slope when Pike suddenly grabbed McConnell's arm in a painful grip.

"What is it?"

"We're not alone out here."

They both dropped down to their bellies again, and the snow beneath them suddenly seemed even colder than it had before.

They scanned the area for a few moments before Pike whispered, "I think I see something."

"What?"

"Look," Pike said, "down near the carcass."

McConnell squinted in an effort to see better. What he saw made his heart leap into his throat. It was the silhouette of a huge shape, and it was moving slowly toward its dead mate.

"Jesus," McConnell said. "It's him."

"He's found his mate," Pike whispered.

"Look at the size of him!"

There was enough moonlight that they were able to

make the bear out clearly. He was nuzzling his dead mate, as if exhorting her to rise.

"If he stays there," McConnell said, "how are we going to get the knife?"

"We'll just have to hope he doesn't stay there."

"How long do we wait?"

"All night, if we have to."

McConnell took no solace in the fact that Koloff would also be waiting all night.

"You ever see two bears mating?" McConnell asked, wearily.

"No."

Pike was lying on his back, trying to get some rest, while McConnell continued to watch the bear. Only an hour had passed and already they were growing numb from the cold. If the bear didn't leave soon they were going to have to move and build a fire somewhere.

"It's really—hey, Pike."

"What?" Pike asked, rolling over.

"He's moving."

The bear, which had been lying quietly by its dead mate for an hour, had gotten to his feet. He circled the dead bear a few times and then finally began to walk away.

"Where do you think he's headed?" McConnell asked.

"Probably to find whoever killed his mate."

McConnell looked at Pike.

"You think bears think about revenge?"

"I'll bet you this one does," Pike said. "Let's wait until he gets good and far away."

They waited for about twenty minutes, and then Pike stood up. As McConnell made to stand Pike put his hand on his shoulder.

"What are you doing?" McConnell asked.

"Stay here."

"Why?"

"If he comes back we'll be out in the open. There's no sense in both of us dying."

"Pike—"

"Also, from up here you'll be able to see him sooner and you can warn me."

That was reasoning McConnell couldn't argue with.

"All right," McConnell said, "but get going, will you? Before he does come back."

"I'm going."

Pike made his way down the rise and across the open ground to the carcass. When he reached it he stared at it for a few moments. Because of the cold, the carcass had not yet begun to stink, but it was an ugly sight, even for someone who had skinned his share of buffalo.

He moved around the huge body, impressed by the size, and by comparison even more impressed with the size of her mate.

Sun Rising had done a fine job of skinning the beast. He knelt down next to it and found the long center incision. The bear was so large that he and McConnell could have slid inside the cut. As it was, he wasn't sure he wanted to stick his hands inside, but if there was a knife in there, he had to know.

Finally, he forced his hand inside the cut. He was surprised at how warm it still was inside. Eventually his hand encountered something hard. He grabbed ahold of it and pulled it out.

It was his knife.

He held it aloft so that McConnell could see. His hand felt colder than the rest of him because he had just pulled it from the warm intestines of the bear.

And that gave him an idea.

"You want to *what?*" McConnell asked.

"You heard me," Pike said. "We need someplace warm to spend the night. We can make a fire, but we're still going to suffer some. We have no blankets and no extra clothing."

"Let me get this straight . . ." McConnell said.

They were standing over the carcass, Pike having waved at McConnell to come down and join him.

"You want the two of us to crawl *inside* this carcass together?"

"If it's being in there together that bothers you, you can go in alone."

"Very funny," McConnell said.

"Look, Skins, stick your hand inside. It's warm, real warm."

"I don't doubt that it is," McConnell said, "but I'm not going to climb inside and wrap myself up in bear intestines."

"Look," Pike said, "we can scoop the intestines out. We'll need to make room for the two of us, anyway. Once that's done it'll be just like crawling under a blanket."

"To you, maybe."

"Okay," Pike said, "come up with another suggestion and I'll listen. We've got to be in shape tomorrow to take on Koloff, Makarov . . . and probably that other bear."

"All right," McConnell said, "all right, so we climb inside this . . . thing. What do we do if the other bear comes back."

"Well . . . there's that risk, but maybe he won't come back."

"Is that supposed to be comforting?"

"No," Pike said, "but it's all we've got. He might come back and not know we're in there. Then again, he might at that."

McConnell stared at his friend then down at the dead bear. Pike noticed that McConnell was shivering. So was he.

"Cold, ain't it?" he said.

"You bastard," McConnell said. "Let's get 'er cleaned out."

Makarov was getting tired of waiting. For a man who prided himself on patience, that was annoying.

"Relax, Uri," Koloff said.

"What if they do not come?"

"They have to come," Koloff said. He was seated by the fire. Makarov was standing, looking off into the darkness. Koloff had a cup of coffee in his hands, enjoying the warmth of it. Next to him was his rifle. "They cannot survive the night."

"Maybe they will just freeze to death."

"Oh, Uri," Koloff said, "now what fun would that be?"

Severance had gone back to his tent voluntarily. Neither Koloff or Makarov were worried enough about him to put Leonid on guard. He knew that if he could find a rifle, he could slip away from camp, find Pike and McConnell, and give it to them.

Who was he fooling? That would take courage, and courage was something he simply did not have.

Sun Rising and Vanya were inside Koloff's tent, waiting for him.

"If he comes in," Vanya said, "we'll have to keep him busy so that if Pike comes back he won't be ready."

"How do we do that?" Sun Rising asked.

"The only way we can," Vanya said, removing her coat and her shirt to reveal her full rounded breasts.

Sun Rising stared at her for a few moments, then started to remove her own clothing. Her breasts were also full, but they were nut brown rather than pale.

"You have a beautiful body," Vanya said.

"So do you."

"I wish my skin was the color of yours."

"You are very lovely the way you are," Sun Rising said. "What do we do if he brings the silent one with him?"

"Then we shall just have to keep them both busy."

It was amazing how many feet of intestines were inside a bear. Pike was glad he had the knife, because he had to cut them here and there to get them all out.

"What do we do with them?" McConnell asked, looking down at them in distaste.

"We'll just have to leave them there," Pike said. He was on his knees, holding open the incision and looking inside. "I think there's room for us now."

"How warm will she stay without all this inside of her?"

"We'll have to find out," Pike said, looking up at his friend. "You ready?"

McConnell made a face and said, "All right, hold the damned thing open."

Chapter Twenty-three

In order for the both of them to get inside the carcass they had to draw their knees up to their chests. It was uncomfortable and it stank, but Pike had been right about one thing—it was warm.

Thanks to the warmth they actually fell asleep.

Pike was the first to wake. Carefully he pulled apart the lips of the incision as if they were the flaps of a tent, and looked outside. It was dawn, and there didn't seem to be anyone around, so he slid through the opening to the ground. Pike shivered and hugged his arms. After the warmth of the carcass the air felt all the colder. He couldn't wait for the sun to come out and warm him.

Packed in as tightly as they were, it was impossible for Pike to get out without waking McConnell, so pretty soon they were both standing on the outside, looking down at the carcass in which they had spent the night.

"Nobody'll believe this," McConnell said.

"You don't think so?" Pike asked. "Now that we've done it, do you really think it hasn't been done before? Think about some of the things we've done—some of the things we've *eaten*—when we were desperate."

"I guess you're right," McConnell said. He looked

down at the carcass and said, "Thanks, old girl."

Pike put his hand on the hilt of his knife, which was back on his hip. It was comforting to have it there.

"What are we going to do now?" McConnell asked.

"We're going to have to find a good place to bushwack those two," Pike said, "and then we're going to have to think of a way to sucker them into it."

"Is that all? We're only dealing with two experienced hunters here."

"They're used to hunting animals," Pike said.

"They've hunted men, according to Severance."

"Maybe so," Pike said, "but those were frightened men, and we're not . . . are we?"

"Hey," McConnell said, "you're the boss. If you say we ain't scared, then we ain't scared."

"You know," Pike said, "I wish you were always this agreeable."

"Enjoy it while it lasts."

During the night Koloff had gotten tired of waiting outside. He had told Makarov that he was going to his tent, and ordered the colonel to alternate watches with Leonid. When Koloff returned to his tent he could not believe his eyes. Two naked, beautiful, willing women were lying in his blankets, and even though he knew why they were there, he decided to take advantage of the situation.

Waking now between them he knew that he had never before spent the night with two more beautiful women, and probably never would again. They must both have really felt something for Pike, because they were very eager in their attempts to distract him. Surely if they had known that Makarov and Leonid were outside on watch they might not have bothered.

181

There was one point during the night when Sun Rising had been seated astride him, riding his rigid cock, and Vanya had been seated on his face so that he could tongue her, when he felt like telling them just to see what their reactions would be. He was, however, having too much of a good time to ruin it, and decided against it.

He sat up now and looked down at both of them. Vanya was asleep on her stomach, her ample rump invitingly raised. Sun Rising was sleeping on her back, her full breasts slightly flattened against her chest. Koloff ran one hand over Vanya's ass and his other over Sun Rising's breasts and belly. He ran his hand along the cleft between Vanya's cheeks until he was able to insert his thumb into her. At the same time he delved into Sun Rising with his middle finger. Neither woman woke, but both grew moist and began to move their hips. Maybe they were dreaming of Pike, because they both started to enjoy themselves.

Vanya began to stir, her eyes fluttering, and Koloff abandoned Sun Rising to position himself behind Vanya. He took hold of her by both hips, raised her ass a little more, and then drove into her cunt from behind. She gasped and came awake, but she was trapped in his grasp.

Sun Rising woke and found herself watching Koloff take Vanya from behind, growling and grunting as he drove into her. She reached out and put her hand on Vanya's head, as if to comfort her. Koloff did not notice the move, but continued to pound away at Vanya with his eyes closed. Vanya, too, had her eyes closed, and tears were running from them.

Sun Rising wished at that moment that she had not left Pike's knife inside the carcass of the bear.

* * *

Makarov, on watch as dawn came, could hear the rutting sounds from inside Koloff's tent. He knew that Koloff was having both women at the same time, and he could not surpress his own erection.

At least it kept him warm.

After Koloff finished with Vanya he stood up, his cock still half erect, and stared down at Sun Rising. She glared at him and then lay down on her back, spreading her legs for him.

"Not this morning, my pretty squaw," he said to her. He felt elated by the night's activities. He began to dress, talking to both of them.

"I have to go out now and hunt Pike down. After I kill him I will bring parts of him to you both so that you may save them. I will also tell him how willing you were to give yourselves to me on his behalf."

Vanya wanted to spit at him, but she did not have the strength to turn around.

"I am sure he will appreciate your offerings," Koloff continued. He paused before leaving the tent, then added, "I know I did."

As he left Vanya began to cry and Sun Rising held her. They didn't even notice that their naked bodies were pressed together. There was nothing sexual in their contact. They simply sought to comfort one another.

Outside Koloff saw that Leonid had started the coffee. Before getting a cup he walked over to where Makarov was sitting.

"Anything?"

"Nothing," Makarov said. "There was not a move all

night."

"Ah, Pike is smart," Koloff said. "He knew we would be waiting for him to come back. Move and counter-move."

"And what is our move now?" Makarov asked.

"We will have to go out and hunt them, after all," Koloff said. "That is, if they did not freeze to death overnight."

"I will get the horses."

"Have some breakfast first, Uri," Koloff said. "We must be well fed before we start the hunt."

With that Koloff walked to the fire, poured himself a cup of coffee, and instructed Leonid to cook bacon for breakfast.

"A lot of it," he said. "I want them to smell it, wherever they are."

"I smell bacon," McConnell said.

"Koloff is shrewd," Pike explained. "He's probably making Sun Rising or Leonid cook all the bacon they have, just to make sure the smell will travel to us."

"I'm going to kill him with my bare hands," McConnell growled.

"We haven't got all that much else to work with," Pike said, "do we?"

Chapter Twenty-four

When Sun Rising and Vanya came out of Koloff's tent they did so with eyes averted. They did not want to look at the man.

"Come to the fire," Koloff called, "and have some breakfast."

To anyone who didn't know what had happened inside the tent that night, it would seem that he was being kind.

As the women approached the fire Koloff got up and said to Makarov, "Saddle the horses. Leonid, you stay here with Severance."

Leonid nodded.

"If Pike or McConnell comes back this way, fire a shot," he instructed further. "We will hear it."

Leonid nodded again.

"And by no means allow them to get their hands on a gun. Do you understand?"

"I understand."

Koloff stood there for a moment looking down at Leonid.

"I do not think I like your attitude, my old friend," he said finally.

Leonid looked up at him and said, "I am sorry if that is so."

"But you will not change it, eh?"

Leonid did not answer.

"Ah, never mind," Koloff said. "Soon things will be back to normal for us. You will see."

"I will see," Leonid replied.

Koloff looked at the two women and ordered, "Eat your breakfast and then clean up. Vanya, I want my tent cleaned and aired out by the time I return."

"Yes."

"Sun Rising, you will continue to work on my bearskin."

"Yes."

"This is such a cooperative group of people, eh?" Koloff said to Makarov.

Makarov didn't answer.

"And where is our fine government escort, Mr. Severance?"

"He is in his tent," Leonid said.

"Perhaps that is a good place for him," Koloff said. "When we return from our successful hunt, we will have to decide what to do with him. Come, Uri. Let us get those horses saddled. If Pike and McConnell are still alive, they are probably freezing and praying that we will soon find them."

"It's damned cold out here," McConnell complained.

"Don't complain," Pike said. "It'll probably get colder."

"Where the hell are they?"

They had found what they thought was a good vantage point, a high ledge among some rocks that afforded them good cover from everything but the cold.

"They're in no hurry, Skins," Pike said. "As far as they know, we could have frozen to death overnight."

"We would have if not for that dead she-bear," McConnell said. "It was a good idea, Pike, but Jesus, I can still smell her on me."

Pike could smell her too, but he didn't mind stinking as long as he was alive.

"Well, one thing for sure," Pike said.

"What?"

"Her mate won't smell us."

"No," McConnell said. "If he smells anyone it'll be Koloff and Makarov, won't it?"

"From up here we'll be able to see whoever passes below, the bear or our Russian friends."

"Friends?" McConnell said, snorting. "We should have known something was wrong the minute we met them."

"Why?" Pike asked, laughing shortly. "They saved our bacon, didn't they?"

"Yeah, they did," McConnell said, "so they could fry it themselves. Do you think he planned this all along?"

"No," Pike said after a minute, "I think he decided it soon after, but I don't think he planned it right from the beginning."

Both men were leaning on their hands, elbows resting on the cold rock.

"Probably decided after you beat him shooting," McConnell suggested.

"Are you blaming me for this?"

"No," McConnell said, "except that you could have let him win."

"I don't shoot to lose, Skins, you know that."

"I know, I know . . ." McConnell said, but a few moments later he added, "You could have bent your principles just once, though."

"Skins . . ."

"All right, forget it," McConnell said.

187

He turned around, sat on the ground, and put his hands close to the small fire they had built. They had found a place where some buffalo had been for awhile and collected some dried chips. They built a very small fire, one that would not attract attention but that would at least allow them to warm their hands—or their butts.

"Did it ever occur to you that this might be pretty damned hopeless?" McConnell asked.

"No."

"Why not?"

Pike looked over his shoulder at his friend and said, "I don't think that way."

McConnell let a couple of beats go by and said, "Yeah, neither do I."

Vanya and Sun Rising sat together by the fire while Leonid prowled the camp. Charles Severance remained inside his tent.

"If we could get a rifle," Vanya said, "and a horse, you could take the rifle to Pike."

"Why me?"

"Come now, Sun Rising, between the two of us who is the better horsewoman—especially in this terrain?"

"You are a fine horsewoman, but you are right. How do we get them, though? Leonid will not give them to us, will he?"

"No."

"He does not look like he approves of what is happening."

"He doesn't," Vanya said, "but he will not go against Ivan."

"Will Mr. Severance help?"

"I am afraid not," Vanya said. "Mr. Severance is a

coward, as he himself will tell you."

"Every man wants a chance to prove that he has courage."

"Not this one, I am afraid," Vanya said.

"Maybe you should talk to him."

Vanya looked over at Severance's tent for a few moments, then said, "I suppose it would not hurt to try, would it?"

"It never hurts to try."

"Perhaps while I am talking to Severance, you should talk to Leonid."

"I will try to keep his attention."

"If he were a different kind of man," Vanya said, "it would be simple to keep his attention."

"I do not understand."

Vanya looked at Sun Rising and said, "Leonid does not like women. He thinks they are a nuisance."

"I see," Sun Rising said, not sure that she did. She knew of men who preferred the intimacy of other men to that of women, but she had never known a man who actually disliked women.

"You go first," Vanya said.

Sun Rising nodded, poured a cup of coffee, and took it to Leonid. She maneuvered around so that Leonid was standing with his back to Vanya. Meanwhile Vanya rose and walked to Severance's tent and entered without announcing herself.

For some reason Severance's pants were down around his ankles, his shorts were halfway down his thighs, and he was scratching his genitals with his right hand. Vanya stood there, boldly looking him over. It surprised her to find that he was so well endowed. When he saw her he gasped and groped for his shorts. In trying to pull them up quickly he staggered, tripped on his pants, and fell heavily to the ground.

189

She looked down at him and said, "I want you to help me."

"Me?" he said from the floor. "What can I do?"

He hadn't got his shorts up and she could see that his penis was becoming erect. She knew this was the effect she had on men, but she had long ago decided that Severance didn't like women. Not the way Leonid didn't like them. Leonid simply preferred the company of men and found anything that a woman had to say trivial. Severance, on the other hand, really *preferred* men, in every sense. Or so she thought.

Looking now at his penis, she realized that she had been wrong.

As he started to rise she said, "Don't get up."

She went over and knelt next to him and very gently put her hand on his chest.

"What do you want?"

"I told you," she said, sliding her hand down his chest, "I want your help."

"To do what?"

"To save Pike."

"I c . . . can't . . ." he said, but he stopped as her hand delved lower. Suddenly she was holding his penis, which was fully erect now. She stroked it, squeezed it, and Severance closed his eyes.

"I want you to help me," she whispered. Leaning close so that her lips almost touched his ear, she said, "Will you?"

Severance shuddered as her hand stroked his cock.

"Y . . . yes."

Minutes later Severance said to her, "I can't do that!"

"Why not?"

"I . . . I'm not that brave," he said "I . . . I could

190

get lost out there."

"Charles," she said, "would you like me to make love with you?"

Severance stared at her beautiful face and said, "Yes." He had never realized until this moment how much he wanted her. He had never thought it possible that he could have her. Not with men like Koloff and Pike around.

"I would make love with you if you would do this for me."

"I could get killed out there," Severance repeated.

Vanya smiled and said, "Would you like to make love before you go?"

"H . . . how could you be sure I would do it, then?"

She fondled his balls in her hand and said, "I would trust you."

Severance was thinking it over when the flap of his tent was thrown back and Leonid stuck his head inside.

"What are you—" he started, then stopped when he saw Severance lying on the floor and Vanya kneeling next to him, the man's genitals in her hand. "Oh . . ."

"Is there something you want, Leonid?" Vanya asked.

"No, I . . . I was just . . . uh, no . . ." Leonid backed out of the tent and allowed the flap to fall closed.

Vanya looked at Severance and said, "See? Now we have time."

She looked at Severance's penis, which she thought was very lovely. She lowered her head and took him into her mouth, still fondling his testicles. He moaned and lifted his hips as her head bobbed up and down on him. It did not take long before he exploded, roaring out loud as he did.

After a few moments she lifted her head and smiled at him.

191

"God!" he said.

"Will you help?"

"Vanya . . ." he said weakly.

She touched him again and said, "This was just the beginning, my love. If you help me, there will be more . . . much more."

She fondled him, and amazingly he began to grow erect again. It was as much a surprise to him as it was to her.

"I will help you," he said at last.

She leaned forward and kissed him and whispered, "I will be back later."

Severance watched her leave, then fell onto his back and just lay there, feeling drained but excited. Never had he had a woman as beautiful as Vanya, and right now he didn't care what he had to do for her.

Was this courage, he wondered? Or just plain foolishness?

Chapter Twenty-five

When Vanya got outside she saw Leonid looking at her strangely. Maybe, she thought, he didn't really dislike women after all. Maybe he was wondering if he could have her. After all, if Charles Severance could have her, maybe anyone could.

She walked to the fire and sat next to Sun Rising.

"I am sorry," Sun Rising said. "I held his attention as long as I could."

"It is all right," Vanya said, smiling.

"Why are you smiling?"

Vanya told Sun Rising what had happened inside Severance's tent.

"How could you do that?" Sun Rising asked.

"It was easy," Vanya said. "He was really quite lovely and he was very passive. I think I know now how Ivan felt when he forced us."

"Is it a good feeling?"

"No," Vanya said, "but it is a better feeling than when Ivan is abusive."

"Why did you do it?"

"He agreed to help us help Pike."

"I see," Sun Rising said. "If he did not have the

courage before, now at least he will do it for you."

"For promises I made him," Vanya said, "and promises I will keep. I will go back to him later with our plan."

"What *is* our plan?" Sun Rising asked.

"We haven't thought of one yet, have we?"

"No, we have not."

"Then we had better think of something quick."

Leonid was confused. Vanya was Koloff's woman and yet there she was with Severance in his tent. How long had this been going on? And should he tell Koloff what he saw? If he did, the man might kill Vanya or Severance or both of them, and there was certainly enough killing going on as it was.

Leonid wished he was back in Russia.

"Stop," Koloff said.

"What is it?" Makarov asked.

"Look."

Makarov looked down at the ground where Koloff was pointing. There were tracks in the snow.

"Bear tracks," Makarov said.

Koloff dismounted and knelt by the tracks. The snow was so hard there was no way he could tell how old the tracks were.

"Well?" Makarov asked.

"Well what?"

"Are they the tracks of our bear or are they the tracks of another?"

Koloff looked up at Makarov and said, "They are old tracks."

Koloff remounted.

"Are you sure?"

Koloff looked at Makarov and said, "We are hunting two men, not a bear. I killed the bear already."

Makarov stared at Koloff and nodded, then they moved off.

"What happens when Koloff sees fresh bear tracks?" McConnell asked.

"In this snow," Pike said, "maybe he won't be able to tell if they're fresh or not."

"And if he does?"

Pike shrugged.

"Then he'll know there's another bear. He'll have to make a choice. Keep hunting us, hunt the bear, or pull up stakes and leave."

"Two of those choices favor us."

"I know."

"One don't."

"I know that, too."

"If he pulls up stakes, where does that leave us?"

"Out in the cold."

"Very funny."

"He won't pull up stakes," Pike said. "He wants this too bad."

"You mean he wants *you* too bad."

"I guess that's what I mean."

McConnell rolled over and supported himself on his elbows. Pike was seated at the fire, which was dying. There was nothing they could do about that; they were out of buffalo chips.

"What's it like?" McConnell asked.

"What's what like?"

"Being you," McConnell said. "I never asked you that before."

"What are you talking about?"

Pike got up from the fire and went to where he could see below.

"I'm serious," McConnell said.

"You know what it's like—"

"I don't know what it's like to be a man women want. A man men want to be like. A man whose name is mentioned in the same breath as Jim Bridger and Kit Carson. I don't know what that's like, Pike."

"Well," Pike said, his tone annoyed, "neither do I."

"Come on," McConnell said. "There's just the two of us here, and who knows if we'll ever get off this rock alive. Come on, tell me. What's it like being you?"

"Sometimes," Pike said, "like now, for instance, it's a pain in the ass."

"Really?"

"How would you like men always wanting to fight you just because of your size? Just because they want to know if you're as tough as you are big."

"But you are."

"I wasn't always," Pike said. "I had to make myself that way. Skins, I wouldn't mind going through the rest of my life without ever having another fight."

"But you fight so good," McConnell said. "I wish I could fight like that."

"You're a pretty good scrapper, Skins."

"Not like you. No, not like you, my friend. And what about the women?"

"The women," Pike said, shaking his head. "Most of them want to know if you're big all over, that's all."

"But you like it?"

"I like women, Skins, there's no denying it, but I can go a long time without one. You know that.

We've both done it."

"I can't do that so easy," McConnell said. "I dearly love women, Pike."

"I know you do, Skins."

"I wish I was with a warm, willing woman right now," McConnell said, "in a warm bed."

"So do I, Skins," Pike said. "So do I."

A half an hour later McConnell was trying to warm his hands by the heat of the ashes. The fire had gone out and the air had grown even colder.

"Skins," Pike said from his vantage point on the rock.

"What?"

"Here they come."

McConnell moved away from the remnants of the fire and joined Pike. Sure enough, he saw two riders down below.

"If we had rifles," McConnell said, "we could pick them off clean as you please."

"But we don't."

"So what do we do now?" McConnell asked. "Throw snowballs at them?"

"Well," Pike said, "we have an advantage. We know where they are and they don't know where we are."

"Big deal," McConnell said. "They still have guns. And we don't . . ."

Pike looked at McConnell.

"We could go back to camp."

"Leonid is there," McConnell reminded him. "Now, he's a fine fella, but if we show up in camp he's sure to blow our heads off."

"Maybe we can get into camp without him seeing us," Pike said. "What do you think?"

"Well," McConnell replied, looking down at the two men, "the camp is in the opposite direction from them. We'd probably have a couple of hours to figure out a way in."

"That's what I figure," Pike said.

"Well, what are we waiting for then?"

When Vanya returned to Severance's tent he was waiting for her. He had his blankets spread out on the floor.

"You are eager," she said.

"Yes, I am," Severance said. "I know why you're doing this, Vanya."

"Oh? Why?"

"Because of Pike," Severance said.

She unbuttoned her shirt so that he could see her firm breasts.

"And you still want me?"

He moistened his lips and said, "By God, what man wouldn't?"

She removed her shirt and he stared at her breasts. When she kicked her pants away he caught his breath. She knelt down next to him and removed his shirt and pants, then pulled the blankets over them. When he felt the weight of her breasts on his chest and the warmth of her hand on his penis, he almost came right there and then.

"I've never been with a woman like you," he said into her hair.

"You will do fine," she assured him, rubbing her hand over his belly, and then moving it lower to wrap her fingers in his pubic hair.

She kissed his chest, licked his nipples, then slid her thigh over him and mounted him.

"Oh, God . . ." he gasped as she took him inside her. "You're so *hot!*"

"And you are so hard," she crooned to him.

She sat astride him, wrapped her hands in his hair, and began to ride him. He reached for her breasts and kneaded them in his hands, then pulled her down so he could suck her nipples. Finally, when he could stand it no longer, he exploded inside of her and she rode him wildly, scratching his chest, using love words on him, speaking English *and* Russian to him, urging him on, making him feel like a real man for the first time in his life . . .

Later she lay with her head on his chest. His hands roved over her, touching her, feeling her. He couldn't believe that she was here with him, and he had to keep his hands on her to reassure himself that it was really happening.

In a low voice, she outlined her plan, the one she and Sun Rising had come up with over the course of the past few hours. He listened intently to what she was telling him. It still had not really hit him that she was talking about something that *he* would be doing.

"Can you do it?" she asked finally. "Can you . . . darling?"

When she said "darling" she ran her hand down over his soft belly to his genitals and began to fondle them.

"I can do it," Charles Severance said. "I'm *sure* I can do it."

"We will get you the gun and the horse," Vanya said. "They will be right outside the back of your tent. Just slit an opening in the tent, go out, and ride."

"What if I can't find Pike?"

"You will find him," Vanya said, "or he will find you, do not worry."

Chapter Twenty-six

It was three hours till sunset, but neither Sun Rising nor Vanya were thinking about that. Nor were they thinking of what would happen to Severance once darkness fell, or of what Koloff would do to them when he came back and found that Severance was gone. All they knew was that they had to do *something* to help Pike—without even knowing if Pike and McConnell were still alive.

Sun Rising had cooked some bacon and beans, and the smell attracted Leonid's attention. He came to the fire to have some, and Vanya stood up to leave.

"Where are you going?" Leonid asked.

"Do you really want to know?" she asked.

She started to walk past him when he grabbed her arm. She stared down her nose at him.

"What would happen if I told Ivan?"

"What would happen," she asked, "if I told Ivan that you touched me?"

"Touched you?" Leonid said, frowning. "What about Severance? What has he done?"

"I will deny it," Vanya said. "When I am lying naked with Ivan, who will he believe, you or me?"

"He will believe me," Leonid said.

Vanya forced herself to smile and then said, "Well then, you go ahead and tell him."

"I do not understand this," Leonid said, shaking his head, but he released her arm.

"Never mind," Sun Rising said to him. She held a plate of bacon and beans out to him. "Eat."

He accepted the plate from her, but he continued to shake his head in bewilderment.

Vanya walked across the camp, and when she was sure that Leonid was not watching she slipped into Colonel Makarov's tent. She looked around quickly, knowing that Makarov owned many guns. Finally she found a pistol and a rifle. They looked American, so they might even have belonged to Pike or McConnell.

She went to the tent flap and looked outside. Leonid was still seated at the fire with his back to her. Noiselessly she hurried from the tent and went to where the horses were tethered.

Vanya was very good with horses, and she managed to loose one of them while crooning to it, keeping it gentled and quiet. She walked the horse around behind Severance's tent and left it there with the guns, then returned to the horses and grabbed a saddle she thought was Severance's. She carried it behind the tent, then hurried round to the front of the tent and entered.

Severance looked up. From the look on his face she knew that there was a possibility that he had changed his mind.

She knelt in front of him and took his hands in hers.

"I want to tell you something."

"What?"

"I meant to sleep with you for Pike's sake."

"I know that, but—"

She pressed two fingers to his lips to silence him.

"Darling, after being with you, I want no other man," she said, trying to sound as sincere as she possibly could.

"What are you saying?" he asked, his eyes wide.

"I am saying I love you. If you do not want to do this, you do not have to."

He frowned now, puzzled.

"You don't want me to go?"

"I do not want you to get hurt," she said. "It is too dangerous, and you mean too much to me now."

She saw the look on his face change and knew she had won.

Now he took her hands in his and kissed them.

"No, I said that I would do this for you, and I will," he said. "When I come back, then we will be together, no matter what anyone says."

She kissed him, pressing her tongue between his lips, a kiss full of promise, and meant to fill him with courage.

"I will stay in here so that Leonid thinks we are together."

"Yes," Severance said, standing. "That is wise."

He picked up a small knife that he still carried and walked to the back of the tent. He pushed the point of the knife into the fabric and then brought it down slowly, tearing the fabric as he went. Inside the tent the noise sounded incredibly loud, but Vanya knew that it could not be heard outside.

That done, Severance put the knife away and turned to look at her.

"Hurry back," she said.

"I will," he said, then added, "darling."

As Severance disappeared Vanya was suddenly struck with the enormity of what she had done. She had seduced the poor man into doing something he would never normally have done, something he might get killed doing.

She fervently hoped that she had done the right thing, and that it would all turn out right in the end.

Severance quietly saddled his horse, then picked up the rifle and pistol. He tucked the pistol into his belt, carried the rifle in one hand, and led the horse with the other. When he felt he had walked the animal far enough away from camp, he mounted up and started riding.

He did not have the slightest idea where he was going.

When Vanya finally came out of Severance's tent she pretended to be adjusting her clothing. She walked to the tent, nodded to Sun Rising, and then sat down next to Leonid. She accepted a plate of food from Sun Rising and started to eat.

Leonid turned his head and looked at her, then tossed the remainder of the coffee in his cup into the fire and walked away, still shaking his head in disbelief.

"Is it done?" Sun Rising asked.

"It is done," Vanya said. "Now we must hope."

Still wondering what was going on, Leonid made a

circuit of the camp and then went to check the horses. By this time Charles Severance had been gone half an hour.

As soon as Leonid saw the missing horse he hurried back to camp. It did not occur to him that someone from camp had taken the horse. He suspected that Pike or McConnell had returned and stolen one.

As he ran into camp both women looked up. They knew at once that he had discovered the missing horse.

"What is wrong?" Vanya asked.

"A horse is missing," he said.

"Perhaps it got loose?" she suggested.

"No, it was taken," Leonid said. "Either Pike or McConnell must have returned and taken it." He looked around and said, "I wonder if they stole a gun."

"Leonid—"

"Wait," he said, and hurried away.

They watched while he searched first Koloff's tent, then Makarov's.

When he came out Vanya asked, "Did they get a gun?"

Leonid said slowly, "I cannot be sure." Suddenly a new look came over his face. He looked directly at Vanya.

"Where is Severance?"

Vanya shrugged, trying to appear as innocent as possible, and said, "In his tent, I assume."

As Leonid started for Severance's tent she called out, "Surely you don't suspect him—" but he didn't stop.

Vanya sat down next to Sun Rising, so close that

205

their shoulders were touching, and together they waited for Leonid to reappear.

When Leonid entered Severance's tent and found it empty he knew immediately what had happened. He searched the tent and found the tear in the back.

Charles Severance would never had done this on his own — *never!*

He left the tent and walked purposefully to the fire.

"This was foolish, Vanya, very foolish."

She didn't bother to deny it.

"Leonid, you don't approve of what Ivan is doing any more than I do —"

"It does not matter," he said, cutting her off. "He is the master."

"Leonid —"

"You seduced Severance and sent him out there to be killed," he said to her, his tone accusing. "When Ivan comes back . . ."

"Are you going to tell him?" she asked.

He looked down at her and said, "He would surely kill you."

She looked up at him with wide eyes and said, "Then, Leonid, my life is in your hands. Do with it what you will."

"He would have to kill me, also," Sun Rising said. "I helped."

Leonid stared at the both of them for a long time, then sat down.

"You have put me in a very difficult position."

"Why?" she asked. "You do not like me, I know that. Why not just tell Ivan?"

"There has been enough killing."

"That is what I say, Leonid, but would you say that to Ivan?"

He didn't answer.

Instead he said to Sun Rising, "May I have a cup of coffee, please?"

Leonid had some thinking to do . . .

Chapter Twenty-seven

It was growing dark as Pike and McConnell made their way toward the camp. The cold was biting into them, making the flesh of their face and hands numb. They had long since stopped talking to each other. It was just too damned cold to talk.

Now, as the darkness deepened, so did the cold. They pulled their hats down as low over their faces as possible, while still allowing them to see. Both were struggling not to give in to the hopelessness of their situation. If they could only reach the camp before the cold killed them—and while Koloff and Severance were still away—but they both knew that wasn't going to happen. By the time they got there the Russians would surely be back.

But even as their minds came close to admitting all of this, they kept walking. Their instinct for survival kept them going and would continue to do so until their legs gave out . . .

Koloff and Makarov were almost back to camp when they thought they saw some movement off to their right.

"What is it?" Makarov asked.

"It's too dark to see."

"Is it them?"

"Judging from the silhouette I saw, I doubt it," Koloff said.

Makarov looked at Koloff. "Another bear?"

"It is possible."

"You were wrong about the tracks."

"I said it was possible," Koloff snapped testily. "It could also have been a buffalo or some other large creature."

"Just the same," Makarov said, "I am not anxious to go and take a look . . . not in the dark."

"On that," Koloff said, "we are agreed, Uri."

Severance was in a panic.

He had no idea where he was, and even if he wanted to turn back, he would not have known in which direction to go.

He was totally lost, bitterly cold . . . and not even the thought of Vanya's body could comfort him.

In fact, he was beginning to think that he was a fool. How could Vanya love him over Koloff or Pike? No, she had simply wanted him to do something for her, and like a lamb led willingly to the slaughter he had done it.

No, he was not beginning to feel the fool . . . he *was* a fool.

And in five minutes, he would be a dead one.

"How far from camp do you think we are?" McConnell asked, his mouth almost touching Pike's ear. If Koloff and Makarov were nearby, they didn't want to be overheard.

"I'd have to take a guess," Pike said. "Half an hour, maybe."

Ten minutes on horseback, McConnell guessed to himself, maybe less. Five.

They stopped suddenly as they spotted something up ahead.

It appeared to be a man and a horse, lying in the snow. As they got closer they saw that both were bloody, torn to pieces by savage jaws.

"The bear's work," McConnell said.

Pike squinted, trying to make out a face in the moonlight.

"Can you make out who it is?" McConnell asked.

"No," Pike said, "but whoever he is he may have done us a favor."

"What favor?"

Pike looked at McConnell and said, "Let's look around for a weapon."

"Ah," McConnell said, and they both began to search the area.

McConnell didn't have long to search. He found a Kentucky pistol in the dead man's waistband. He removed it, then examined it closely.

"Pike!" he called excitedly.

Pike came up to him, carrying a rifle he had found several yards from the dead man.

"Skins," Pike said, "you'll never believe what I've found."

"Your pistol," McConnell said, holding the pistol aloft.

"And your rifle," Pike said, showing the weapon to McConnell.

They both looked carefully at the body now, examining the clothes.

"It's not Leonid," McConnell said at last.

"It can't be . . . Severance, can it?" Pike asked in disbelief.

They both knelt over the bloody carcass, heedless of the fact that their knees were soaking up blood from the snow.

"This is the horse Severance was riding," McConnell said.

Pike turned the man's head toward him. The throat had been torn out and the head was barely connected to the body, but the face, though streaked with claw marks, was undoubtedly that of Charles Severance.

"What the hell was he doing out here?" Pike asked.

"Who knows?"

"Did he suddenly get brave?"

"I find that unlikely," McConnell said. "What could make a coward like this a brave man?"

"What can make any coward a brave man?"

They exchanged glances and then McConnell said, "A woman?"

"A woman."

"Which one?" McConnell wondered.

"That doesn't matter," Pike said. "Look around for a powder horn."

They searched for the horn, going so far as to move the body of the horse in the hope that it was underneath.

Sure enough, it was, but it had been crushed by the weight of the horse, the powder pounded into the snow . . . useless.

"Damn!" Pike said. "One shot in the rifle, one in the pistol. That's all we have."

"It's more than we had a little while ago," McConnell said. "Let's make the best of it."

"You're right," Pike said.

They both stood, suddenly heartened.

"If we pick up the pace we might make the camp in twenty minutes."

"We might even work up a sweat," McConnell said.

"God forbid," Pike said. "The cold would freeze it, and us, solid."

They exchanged weapons. Pike put the pistol inside his belt; McConnell held the rifle in his right hand.

"Let's get this over with once and for all," Pike said. They started toward the camp on the run, both hoping they wouldn't run into the bear. Two shots were plenty to take care of two men, but they doubted they would be enough to dispose of the bear.

When Koloff and Makarov rode back into camp the tension in the air was almost thick enough to defy the cold.

Leonid stood silently at the fire and watched them ride in. It was obvious that they had not found what they were looking for.

Vanya and Sun Rising remained seated by the fire. They were watching Leonid rather than Koloff, both wondering what he was going to tell his master—and what his master's reaction would be.

Leonid approached the two riders and accepted the horse's reins.

"Nothing?" Leonid asked.

"No," Makarov said. He was clearly dissatisfied with their progress.

Leonid was looking at Koloff, however, and not at Makarov.

"Pike is good," Koloff said. "He is very good." He did not seem dissatisfied, but Leonid knew better. He had been with Koloff a long time, and he knew when the man looked worried. He had only seen that look once or twice over the years, but he was seeing it again.

If Pike had Koloff worried now, wait until he found out about Severance . . . and the missing weapons.

Chapter Twenty-eight

Vanya and Sun Rising watched as Leonid entered Koloff's tent. They were still wondering what Leonid was going to tell him when Makarov suddenly came rushing out of his own tent.

"He has discovered the missing weapons," Vanya said. "We will have to deal with this now, no matter what Leonid tells him."

Koloff listened to what Makarov had to say about the missing weapons and then turned to Leonid.

"And you think Severance took the weapons when he left?"

"Why else would he have left?" Leonid asked.

"Just to get away?" Makarov asked.

Koloff considered this and then shook his head.

"If he were going to run he would have done it a long time ago."

"Then why did he do it now?" Makarov asked. "And take two weapons with him?"

"What did he take?" Koloff asked.

"McConnell's rifle and Pike's pistol."

"A powder horn and shot?"

"Yes."

"Damn!" Koloff said. "He must have taken it with the thought of finding Pike and McConnell."

"We are still facing the same question," Makarov said. "Even if he wanted to help them, why would he decide to do it now?"

"He did not decide on his own," Koloff said. "Someone put the idea into his head."

"But why would he do it?" Makarov asked. "The man's a coward. Even if someone else gave him the idea, where would he get the courage to do it?"

Koloff looked from Makarov to Leonid to Makarov again and said, "Where does any man get courage?"

There was a moment of silence and then Makarov said, "From a woman."

"Yes."

"But which one was it?" Makarov asked. "The squaw or Vanya?"

"Not Sun Rising," Koloff insisted. "It would not even occur to her."

"Vanya?" Makarov said. "Why would she do it?"

"She likes Pike," Koloff explained, "and it would not be hard for her to wrap a man like Severance around her little finger."

"If Severance finds them, they'll be armed now," Makarov said.

"That will make the hunt more interesting," Koloff said.

"The damn hunt is already more interesting than it should have been," Makarov burst out fervidly. "They should not have been able to avoid us for two days."

"Maybe they haven't," Koloff said. "Maybe they're dead. And maybe Severance will be dead before the night is out. Then all of our problems will be solved. Of course, not the solution I was looking forward to, but after all, I did get my bear."

"And that is another thing to consider," Makarov said, "the presence of the second bear."

"Another bear?" Leonid asked.

"There *might* be another bear," Koloff said. "We do not know that for certain."

"Ivan—"

"Uri," Koloff said, "I think I would like to talk to Vanya now."

"Do you think she will admit it?"

"Vanya is a strong woman," Koloff said. "I do not think she will deny it. Leonid?"

"Yes?"

"Ask Vanya to come in, will you?"

"Yes."

"Leonid?"

"Yes?"

"You did not know anything about this, did you?"

"No," Leonid said, "I did not." In a way, this was the truth. He did not know anything about it until after it was done.

Koloff stared at Leonid for a few moments.

"All right," Koloff said finally. "Have Vanya come in."

When Leonid approached the fire both Sun Rising and Vanya looked up at him.

"What did you tell him?" Sun Rising asked.

"Nothing," Leonid said.

"Nothing?" Vanya insisted.

"I told him the truth: that weapons, a horse, and Severance were missing. He drew his own conclusions from that."

"And?" Vanya asked.

Leonid hesitated and then said, "He wants to see

you, Vanya."

"Just Vanya?" Sun Rising asked.

"Yes."

"I will go with you," the Indian woman said.

"No," Vanya said, "I will go alone."

"His anger—"

"I will be able to handle him," Vanya replied. She took Sun Rising's hand and squeezed it, then walked away from the fire toward Koloff's tent.

"Is he angry?" Sun Rising asked.

"He is."

"Will he kill her?"

"I do not think so."

Sun Rising hesitated a moment, then asked, "Can she . . . handle him?"

Leonid took his time before answering. "I do not think so."

When Vanya entered the tent Koloff said, "You can leave, Uri."

"Ivan—"

"Uri!"

Makarov stared at Koloff for a few moments, then left the tent, holding himself stiff and straight.

"Tell me why, Vanya." Koloff ordered.

"For Pike."

"That simple?"

"There has been enough killing, Ivan."

"That is funny," he mused. "I thought I was the best judge of that."

"Not anymore," she replied. "Not for a long time. Your judgment left you a long time ago."

"And yet you stayed?"

"Perhaps my judgment has not been very good

217

either," she admitted.

"Did you make Severance feel like a man before getting him to do your bidding?"

She lifted her chin and said, "I am not proud of that, but I felt it was necessary."

"Really?"

Vanya did not answer.

"Tell me," Koloff asked, "how did you expect me to react to this?"

"Angrily."

"Well, you were correct."

"If you beat me, Ivan," Vanya said, "I will leave."

"Is that supposed to deter me?" he asked. "If I beat you severely, Vanya, you will not be able to walk, let alone leave."

As he stood up she took a step or two back in fear, then steeled herself and waited. He approached her and she managed not to flinch when he touched her face.

"I do not care," he said finally.

"About what?"

"That you sent Pike weapons," Koloff said. "I do not care."

Looking puzzled she asked, "And why not?"

"Because Severance will probably get lost and die before he ever finds Pike."

Vanya debated saying what first came into her mind, then decided to say it anyway.

"Perhaps not."

"Of course, there is the chance that he will find Pike and McConnell, but if he does, I still do not care."

Again she asked, "Why?"

"Because I am a hunter, Vanya, and this adds spice to the hunt."

"Then . . . you do not intend to . . . punish me?" Vanya asked.

"Punish you?" Koloff asked, stroking her cheek. "Of course I intend punish you, dear."

The fear crept back into her eyes and she said, "How?"

"Tomorrow morning," Koloff said, "when we go out to hunt, you will come with us."

"Go with you? Why?"

"Because," Koloff gloated, "when we finally catch up to your friend Pike, I want you to watch me kill him."

Chapter Twenty-nine

Pike and McConnell both saw the fire at the same time.

"We're here," McConnell said, tightening his hand around his rifle.

They moved closer until they could make out the dark shapes of the tents, and could see the people seated at the fire.

"I see Sun Rising and Leonid," Pike said.

"So do I."

"The others must be in the tents."

"Yeah," McConnell said, "but who's in which tent with who?"

"Well," Pike said, trying to get more comfortable lying on the snow, "either they're all in Koloff's tent or Koloff and Vanya are in his tent and Makarov is in his."

"Do you think they know about us? I mean, that we're armed?"

"By now they must know," Pike decided. "I remember Koloff telling Makarov to put the weapons in his tent. By now Makarov must have noticed them missing."

"Since there'll be a powder horn missing," McConnell said, "they'll assume we're fully armed, not that we only have one shot apiece."

"Right."

"Pike," McConnell suggested, "from here you could pick one of them off with the rifle."

"Maybe," Pike said, "but we're too far for an accurate pistol shot."

"I can get closer," McConnell volunteered. "If you make the shot with the rifle, I can make the other with the pistol."

"That would still leave one man," Pike reminded him. "Leonid."

"Providing we take out Koloff and Makarov with our one shot each."

"Why waste a shot on Leonid?"

"Skins, Leonid is not on our side. He's one of the enemy."

"I don't agree," McConnell said. "He may not be on our side, but I can't believe he's on Koloff's."

"Skins, Skins," Pike said, shaking his head, "he serves Koloff."

"He knows Koloff is wrong."

"Do you want to bet your life on him?"

McConnell thought that over and then said, "Maybe I don't, but I still think our best bet is to pick off Koloff and Makarov and worry about Leonid after."

"Don't forget Vanya and Sun Rising," Pike said.

"Well," McConnell replied, "Vanya might be considered one of them, and Sun Rising—well, she's a Crow. Koloff's got no reason to kill her."

"Hey," Pike said, "as far as I'm concerned, he's got no reason to kill us either, but that ain't stoppin' him from trying, is it?"

"No, it ain't," McConnell said. "All right, Pike, call the shot."

Pike hesitated, and then his gaze fell upon Severance's tent.

"There's one tent we know will be empty," he said.

"Severance's?"

"Yeah. If we can get to that tent—"

"One of us."

"Right, if one of us can get to that tent—did he carry a gun?"

"I don't remember."

"There might be something in his tent we can use, but even if there isn't, one of us will be inside the camp. We can certainly do more damage from there."

"All right," McConnell said. "Who goes?"

"I do."

"Why you?"

"I move more quietly than you do."

"But you're a better shot. I should be the one to get closer, so I can be more effective with the pistol."

Pike opened his mouth to argue, but there was no argument he could give. McConnell was right.

"All right," Pike said, "you go."

They exchanged weapons.

"I'll try and signal you when I'm there."

"Nothing too obvious," Pike said. "If you can't signal, I'll assume you're inside. I'll give you . . . five minutes to get set, and then I'll take my best shot."

"All right," McConnell said, getting to his knees. He put his hand out and Pike took it in his.

"Good luck," Pike said.

"Shoot straight."

And McConnell was gone, melting into the darkness. Pike settled down to wait the promised five minutes.

When Sun Rising saw Vanya leave Koloff's tent she breathed a sigh of relief.

"He did not punish her," she said aloud.

222

Leonid looked up and saw Vanya walking toward them.

"He will," he said.

"When?"

"Soon."

Vanya reached them and sat down.

"Thank you," she said to Leonid.

"For what?"

"For not telling."

Leonid shrugged.

"What does that matter? Now he knows."

"But he does not know about Sun Rising's involvement," Vanya said, reaching out and touching the Crow woman's hair. "For that we are thankful."

"That does not matter," Leonid said. "Whether he knows about her or not, you know he will do what he wants to do."

"What does he mean?" Sun Rising asked.

"He means," Vanya said, "that Ivan probably decided a long time ago what he was going to do with you when this is all over."

"What?"

"Who knows?" Leonid said. "It could be anything from taking you back to Russia with him to killing you."

"He would kill me?" she asked. "Why?"

Leonid and Vanya exchanged a glance.

"Why does he want to kill Pike?" Vanya said. "He simply decided that he wanted to. He does as he pleases, Sun Rising."

"I do not understand this man," she said. "My people kill, but with reason. They kill to survive."

"Is that what they were doing to Pike and McConnell when we came along?" Leonid asked. "They were trying to survive?"

"Walking Cat thought they wanted to steal me."

"And did they?" Vanya asked.

"No," Sun Rising said. "I wanted to go with them—with Pike."

"What is it about this man Pike?" Leonid wondered. "He turns you against your people, he turns you, Vanya, against Ivan and Ivan himself is obsessed with killing him."

"He's an extraordinary man," Vanya said.

"To me he is just a man," Leonid replied, "and if he is not already dead, he will die when Ivan finds him."

"Perhaps not," Vanya said. "Perhaps Pike will kill Ivan."

"Perhaps," Leonid agreed, "and then Makarov will kill Pike."

"And McConnell will kill Makarov."

"Or Makarov will kill McConnell."

After listening to both of them Sun Rising asked, "And when does it stop?"

Vanya and Leonid looked at each other. Finally Leonid said, "When there is no one left to kill."

"That sounds mad."

Leonid stared back at her and said, "It is."

McConnell worked his way behind Severance's tent and was considering how to get inside without being seen when he noticed the tear in the fabric. He turned to look for Pike, but there was no way he could see him. Just in case Pike could see him, though, he waved a few times and then slipped into the tent through the cut.

Inside he waited until his eyes became accustomed to the darkness. He could see the campfire flickering against the outside of the tent. When he could see fairly well he started searching, but there was no pow-der or shot to be found anywhere.

Satisfied that there was no point in looking any fur-ther he moved to the front flap and took a peek out-side. From there he could see the fire, and he noticed that Vanya had joined Sun Rising and Leonid there. There was still no sign of Koloff or Makarov. They could each be inside their own tent, or they could both be in one, he couldn't tell.

Makarov's tent was across from Severance's. It oc-curred to McConnell that if the tent was empty, and he could get inside, there'd be plenty of powder and shot to be had.

If it was empty. If it wasn't, and he was caught, his life would be in Pike's hands.

Chapter Thirty

Pike watched the camp. There was no sign of McConnell, but the five minutes were almost up, so he had to assume that he had made it to Severance's tent.

There were still only three people around the fire, and the only one of those three he had to worry about was Leonid. McConnell was right, though. Leonid could not be one of their primary targets. They had to worry about Koloff and Makarov, and then see what happened.

Pike lifted the rifle to his shoulder and sighted down the barrel, trying to pick the best position for him to take the shot. He could see the front of both Makarov and Koloff's tent. As soon as one of them appeared, he'd be able to take a shot.

He was still sighting on Makarov's tent when out of the corner of his eye he saw movement. He lowered the rifle and was surprised to spot McConnell coming out of Severance's tent. He hadn't even seen him go in. He must have gotten in from behind, which meant that was probably how Severance had gotten out.

But what the hell was McConnell doing?

If anyone at the fire had turned around at that moment they would have seen McConnell, but they didn't. They were too deep in conversation.

Pike managed to figure out what McConnell had in mind. If Makarov wasn't in his tent, McConnell would be able to get inside and possibly grab some powder and shot, maybe even another rifle.

He was also taking a chance of being caught or killed. Pike had to admit to himself that it would be better if McConnell were killed instead of caught. A live McConnell could be used against him; if McConnell were killed, Pike would have no one to worry about except himself.

He was hoping it wouldn't come to that.

He watched, his shoulders tight with tension, as McConnell started to cover the distance between the tents.

McConnell knew he was taking a chance, but what did they have to lose? If Makarov was in his tent, McConnell had just as much of a chance of killing the Russian as the Russian had of killing him.

Moving as quietly as he could, he covered the distance quickly until he was standing next to the other tent. There was a light burning inside, but that didn't mean that Makarov was there. There was also a light inside Koloff's tent. In fact, McConnell could see Koloff's shadow. There was no telltale shadow in Makarov's tent.

McConnell removed the pistol from his belt, pushed back the flap of the tent, and slipped in.

Pike watched McConnell run across to the other tent. He could not see his friend's face, but he did see him take the gun out of his belt just before entering the tent.

With McConnell out of sight, Pike suddenly experienced some anxiety. Anything could be happening inside the tent . . .

The moments of silence passed painfully, and then suddenly there were the shots . . .

As McConnell stepped into the tent the light hurt his eyes. The storm lamp was turned up higher than it needed to be, and in a second he found out why.

"Do not move," Makarov said. The voice came from behind him, to the left. Makarov must have been keeping low, to keep his shadow from showing.

McConnell, still squinting at the light, stood stock still, keeping the pistol hidden in front of his body.

"Where is Pike?" Makarov asked.

"Not far behind me."

Makarov laughed.

"Where is the pistol? In your belt?"

"Yes."

"Take it out. Slowly."

McConnell knew he had only one shot. He held the pistol in his left hand and deliberately poked out his right elbow so it would look like he was reaching into his belt for the gun.

Suddenly he spun left, pointing the gun lefthanded, and fired. The move fooled Makarov, whose finger squeezed the trigger a second later than McConnell's.

McConnell's ball struck Makarov in the center of the chest, driving the man back against the side of the tent. The Russian's ball drove through McConnell's right thigh and out the other side. McConnell fell to the ground, but then quickly pushed himself to his feet again. He looked around, trying to block out the pain, trying to locate another weapon, when he saw Pike's rifle. He grabbed it and made for the tent flap . . .

The two shots galvanized Pike into action. Throwing caution to the wind he rose and started running in a straight line toward the camp.

At the sound of the shots, fired so close together they could almost have been one, Leonid, Sun Rising and Vanya all jumped up and started to look around. Leonid grabbed his rifle and held it ready. He looked first at Koloff's tent, then at Makarov's. When he saw the flap of Makarov's tent thrown back, he raised the rifle and aimed . . .

McConnell limped out of the tent and quickly looked toward Koloff's tent. Koloff was not out yet. He turned to point his rifle at the tent flap, when he heard a voice say, "Drop the rifle!"

He looked over at the fire and saw Leonid aiming at him.

Then they all heard the third shot.

Pike saw McConnell come out of the tent, and Leonid point his rifle directly at him.

"Damn!" he said, dropping into a crouch and aiming at Leonid. He could not afford to wait and see if the Russian was going to shoot.

Pike fired . . .

The ball struck Leonid in the torso. He gave a coughing grunt and dropped his rifle, falling toward the two women, who quickly moved out of his way. The body fell to the ground between them.

McConnell saw Leonid fall and turned his attention once more to Koloff's tent. He aimed his rifle at the flap, waiting for the man to appear.

"Drop the gun!" a voice commanded from behind him.

He felt the barrel of a gun pressed to his head, just below his right ear.

"Severance was not the only man who could cut through his tent," Koloff said. "Drop the rifle."

McConnell hesitated a moment, then obeyed.

When Pike saw Koloff step behind McConnell and press his rifle barrel to his friend's ear, he stopped running and fell onto his belly.

His worse fear had come true.

McConnell was now a hostage.

Part Four

Cat and Mouse
. . . and Mouse

Chapter Thirty-one

"Did you kill him?" Koloff asked.

"Who?"

"The colonel, of course."

"What do you think?"

"I think we should go over to the fire and join the others," Koloff said, prodding McConnell in the back with his rifle.

They walked over to where Sun Rising and Vanya were crouched over Leonid.

"He is still alive," Vanya said to Koloff, who didn't seem to care.

"You know, Mr. McConnell," Koloff said, "I could blow your spine out right now—did I say that correctly?—and then it would be only Pike and me."

"Why don't you?"

"I will tell you why," Koloff said. "With a man like Pike I will need an edge."

"And you think I'm your edge?"

Koloff laughed.

"I know you are."

"You think because you have me Pike won't—"

"What I think," Koloff said, poking McConnell hard to interrupt him, "is that Pike will not risk your life. As long as I have you, I have an advantage."

"Then why don't you just call out to him?" McConnell asked. "He's right out there in the dark. Just tell him to come on in or you'll kill me. Go ahead, see what happens."

Koloff risked a look out into the darkness. The silence grew louder and louder until he spoke again.

"Pike!"

No answer.

"Stand over there next to them," Koloff said, pushing McConnell. McConnell stood next to Vanya and noticed that Koloff had his powder horn and possibles bag over his shoulder.

"Ivan," Vanya said, "Leonid is still alive, but he needs help."

"So help him," Koloff said. When Vanya started to lean over the injured man again he snapped, "No, not you . . . let her do it."

Sun Rising looked at Koloff and then bent over Leonid to try and help him.

"You two just stand still," Koloff told Vanya and McConnell.

"Pike!" he shouted again. "I have your friend. I have McConnell."

All that came back was silence.

"See?" McConnell said. "Holding me is going to do you no good."

Koloff looked at McConnell, then raised the barrel of his rifle so that it was pointing directly at his face.

"If that is truly the case," Koloff said, "then there is no need to keep you alive at all."

McConnell pondered that for a moment, then said to Koloff, "On the other hand . . ."

Pike watched Koloff walk McConnell over to the fire.

He heard Koloff calling out to him, but he remained silent, even when the Russian mentioned that he had McConnell. Pike could *see* that he had McConnell.

"You had better come in, Pike," Koloff shouted again. "Or I will kill your friend!"

While he said this Koloff had his rifle pointed at McConnell's face.

Pike got to his feet and ran a diagonal course that took him to Severance's tent. He was going to go through the tear in the back, but stopped when he saw something that gave him an idea.

"No answer," Koloff said. He looked directly at McConnell and said, "I guess your friend is not that concerned for your safety."

McConnell knew that he had to keep Koloff talking to give Pike time to do something.

"Sure he is," McConnell countered, "he's just a little more concerned for his own safety."

"That does not make him much of a friend."

McConnell laughed and stared at Leonid, who was being attended to by Sun Rising.

She looked up at Koloff and said, "I need water and bandages."

Koloff ignored her.

"What about you?" McConnell asked him. "You're more concerned about yourself than you are about your friend here."

"Leonid is not my friend," Koloff said. "He works for me."

"What about Makarov? Maybe I didn't kill him. Maybe he's bleeding in his tent."

"If that is so then he will soon be dead. You see, I never professed friendship to either of these men. All I ask from them is obedience."

"Correct me if I'm wrong," McConnell continued, "but I'll bet you don't have many friends, do you?"

Koloff didn't answer.

"You are right," Vanya said. "He does not."

"Friends are no great asset, as you can plainly see here," Koloff said. "And now I'm afraid I must dispose of you so I may give your *friend* Pike my full attention."

Koloff lifted the rifle and McConnell readied himself to leap across the fire at him, when suddenly there was a loud roar, and a bear charged into camp, heading straight for them.

Stunned, Koloff nevertheless turned quickly to face the charging animal. He had convinced himself that there was only one bear and that he had killed it. It took him only a split second, though, to realize what was happening. He raised his rifle hastily and fired . . .

Even as the bear came charging into camp McConnell noticed that there was something odd about it. It was awfully . . . stringy looking . . .

They all saw Koloff's ball strike the bear, but it didn't seem to slow the animal down . . . Suddenly the animal stopped. It wasn't wounded, but it just stood there. They all stared at it, and then to everyone's surprise it shed its skin. The bearskin fell to the ground and Pike emerged from beneath it, laughing.

"Hello, Koloff," he chuckled. "You missed me."

* * *

It was a calculated risk to leave his rifle behind when he donned the bearskin, but he had no choice. It seemed only fitting that as the carcass had saved their lives once, now the skin was doing the same.

When Koloff fired, Pike felt the ball strike the pelt, but it passed through without harming him. Good. Now Koloff would need time to reload . . .

"Pike?" Koloff said. He stared at Pike for a few moments, then looked down at the bearskin.

"It's all over, Koloff," Pike said.

Koloff looked at Pike again and then threw his rifle at him. As Pike dodged it, Koloff leaped over the fire, slammed into McConnell, and grabbed Vanya by the neck. He produced a knife from his belt and held it to her throat.

"It is not quite over, Pike," the Russian snarled. Without looking he said to McConnell, "Get up and move over next to Pike."

McConnell did as he was told.

"Pike, hand my rifle over the fire to Vanya."

Pike picked up the rifle and held it out until Vanya could take hold of it.

"Now Vanya and I are going to back out of here. If you follow, I will cut her throat. Do you understand?"

"I understand that you have nowhere to go, Koloff," Pike said. "Why not just give up?"

"I have somewhere to go, Pike," Koloff said. "I am going out there, into the darkness, and if you are any kind of a man you will come out there and get me . . . alone."

"And you're taking Vanya with you? Why? She'll only be in your way, slow you down, hamper your movements."

"That is true," Koloff said after a moment. "I will

237

hold her until I have gotten away and then I will release her."

"Or kill her," Pike said.

"That is nonsense," Koloff said, beginning to back away, dragging Vanya with him. "Why would I kill her?"

"Who knows what you'll do or why you'll do it?" Pike asked.

"I give you my word," Koloff said, "I will send her back to you unharmed." He continued to back up until he was swallowed up by the darkness. His disembodied voice called out, "Come and get me, Pike. Come alone . . . if you dare."

"I need water and bandages," Sun Rising said again.

"Skins, get her what she needs," Pike said. "I'll get my rifle."

When McConnell returned Pike was standing over Leonid, his rifle nestled in the crook of his arm. Sun Rising was standing next to him.

She turned to McConnell and said, "It is too late. He is dead."

"I didn't want to kill him," Pike explained, "but he was drawing a bead on you."

"I know," McConnell said.

"What happened with Makarov?"

"He was waiting for me, but he's dead now."

"Lucky for you he didn't—hey!" Pike had just noticed that his friend was wounded. "Jesus, you're bleeding pretty bad."

McConnell looked down at his wound. Up until that moment he'd been running on adrenaline, but now he suddenly felt very weak.

"I am going to need these bandages and water after

all," Sun Rising said.

Pike caught McConnell as he began to sway.

"Sit him down," Sun Rising commanded.

Pike sat McConnell down and tore his friend's pants leg.

"It went right through," Pike said. "Bandage it up good and tight, Sun Rising. He's going to need to ride in the morning."

As Pike stood, McConnell reached out and grabbed his arm.

"Where do you think you're going?"

"I'm going after him."

"That's what he wants."

"Well, what a coincidence," Pike said. "It's what I want too."

Just then Vanya came stumbling into camp.

"Vanya!" Pike said as she crumpled into his arms.

"He let me go," she said as if she couldn't believe it. "He actually let me go."

"Maybe he feels more for you than you realize," Pike said.

"No," she replied, regaining her balance. "No, he sent me back to taunt you. He said he'd be waiting for you . . . out there."

"Well, that's where I'm going."

"You can't," she pleaded. "He'll kill you."

"Pike—" McConnell began, but Pike cut him off.

"Look," he said to all of them, "the way things stand right now I have as much chance of killing him as he has of killing me—maybe even better, since these are my mountains. Besides which, there's a third player in this game."

"The other bear."

"There *is* another bear?"

"The mate," Pike said. "And he's the big one."

"It's out there and you are going to go?" Vanya asked. "Why not leave Ivan and the bear to each other? We can leave in the morning."

"No," Pike said, "it has to end here and now, on this mountain. It was bound to come to this. From the moment we met it was bound to come down to this."

Pike collected a powder horn and some shot, picked up his rifle and headed out into the darkness.

"Pike—" Vanya called.

"Let him go," McConnell said as Sun Rising wrapped a bandage around his leg.

"But—"

"He's right, Vanya," McConnell went on, "it had to come to this. The three of them, out there, playing cat and mouse . . . and mouse."

Sun Rising looked up into McConnell's eyes and asked, "Which of them is the cat?"

Chapter Thirty-two

Even as Pike made his way through the darkness he knew that he was being foolish. Vanya was right. They should have simply left in the morning, leaving Koloff behind to make his own way. Maybe he'd run into the bear and maybe he wouldn't. Maybe he'd just freeze to death, a fate he certainly deserved.

But Pike couldn't leave it at that. Koloff had done too much for him to leave it to fate. Fate was funny; it just might decide to let him get away. But Pike wouldn't do that. He had no intention of letting Koloff get away with anything . . .

When his night vision adjusted, Pike was able to make out the tracks in the snow. First Koloff's and Vanya's, then Vanya's after Koloff released her, finally, Koloff's tracks as he moved away . . . to where? To a place where he thought to make a stand against Pike?

Pike continued walking. It would be simpler if Koloff *was* waiting for him somewhere. It would save Pike the trouble of tracking him down.

Also, the faster they got this confrontation over with, the better chance they'd all have of getting away from here without running into the other bear.

* * *

Ivan Koloff had never felt panic before in his life, so he didn't know what he was feeling now. He knew only that his heart was pounding and that he felt . . . helpless. He still didn't realize that for the first time in his life he was experiencing naked fear.

He did know that he had acted rashly in leaving camp so abruptly and in letting Vanya go. He could have used her against Pike. Now he was out here in the dark, alone, and he had invited Pike to come out and find him.

In daylight Koloff would have retained his confidence. It was the darkness that was causing him to . . . to what? The word *panic* never entered his mind.

He wished he could find some shelter, someplace to spend the night. Then, in the morning, he'd be able to meet Pike on equal terms. Pike knew what it was to spend a night in these mountains; Koloff did not.

He needed somewhere warm to go, and he could only think of one.

Pike stopped walking as something occurred to him. Koloff had never been out in the mountains at night. He'd know that he couldn't hope to outmaneuver Pike in the darkness. He'd have to find someplace to spend the night, find some kind of shelter. Pike knew there was no such shelter in the area. He and McConnell had used the only shelter he knew of, the carcass of the bear, and that would be useless by now.

There was only one other place warm enough to spend the night.

The camp.

"I should have gone with him," McConnell said.

242

"You can't even walk," Vanya said.

"Sure I can walk," McConnell said. He stood up to demonstrate and took a few halting steps, wincing at the pain.

"You are not walking anywhere," Sun Rising insisted.

"Vanya," McConnell said suddenly, "get me a rifle."

"Why?"

"Just get me one," he said. "Check inside Makarov's tent."

"The colonel's tent?" Vanya said, looking dubious.

"Yeah, right over—oh," McConnell said, remembering that Makarov's body was still inside.

Between them Vanya and Sun Rising had dragged Leonid's body to his own tent. Vanya had been reluctant but had finally done her share. Now he was asking her to go and look at another dead body.

"All right," he said, "Pike's pistol should be lying just outside Makarov's tent where I dropped it. See if you can find it."

"All right, but you sit back down."

"Do you think he will come back here?" Sun Rising asked.

"There is no place out there where he can survive the night," McConnell said. "If he does come back, we better be ready for him."

Sun Rising stood up and said, "I will look in the tent for a weapon."

"Fine," McConnell said. "Good idea."

As both women were looking for weapons McConnell stared out into the darkness. The darkness was always an equalizer. In the dark men looked the same, were the same size. Any man had the chance to kill any other man at any given time.

Vanya returned and stopped short when she saw the odd look on McConnell's face.

"What is it?" she asked. When he didn't answer she called out, "Skins!"

He started and stared at her.

"What is wrong?" she asked.

"Nothing," he said, shaking his head. "I was just thinking."

"Of what?"

"Nothing," he said, again. "It would just confuse you. Ah, you found it."

"Yes," she said, handing him the pistol.

At that moment Sun Rising returned holding a rifle, a powder horn, and a possibles bag.

"All right," McConnell said. "Ladies, we are armed, if not well armed."

"But possibly," Ivan Koloff announced, "not in time."

They all turned and stared at Koloff, who had come into camp behind them while they were talking.

"You came back here?" Vanya said. "You are a fool."

"No, I am not. There is no other place for me to spend the night."

"Pike will come back here for you."

"Possibly," he replied, "but not before he wanders around in the dark for a while . . . and this time when he comes back, I will be ready for him."

McConnell stood there with the empty pistol in his hand, feeling helpless and foolish. He knew that he had to do something.

"Sun Rising, put the rifle down," Koloff said. When she hesitated he pointed his rifle at her. She did as she was told.

"Now you, Mr. McConnell. Put the weapon down."

"I don't think so," McConnell said, pointing the pistol at Koloff.

"Come now, Mr. McConnell," Koloff said. "We all know that the pistol is not loaded."

244

"Do we?" McConnell said. "Why don't you try me then, Ivan?"

Koloff stared at McConnell for a few moments, trying to read the man's face.

"You are bluffing."

"If I'm not," McConnell said, "and you fire, we'll both be dead. If I am, and you fire, I'll be dead. Either way, I'm dead, so what do I have to lose?"

Koloff pondered that.

"And consider what you have to lose, Ivan." McConnell added.

Koloff and McConnell stared at each other until the quiet became deafening . . . and then was broken by the sound of a roar.

They all turned and saw it charging into camp . . . and this time there could be no mistake.

This time it was the real bear.

Chapter Thirty-three

Koloff turned and fired immediately. His shot struck the bear high on the right shoulder but did little to slow him down. The bear closed its huge paws around Koloff's body, lifting him up so that his feet kicked at the air.

Ignoring the sound of Koloff's screams, McConnell moved immediately.

"Split up," he shouted at the women.

"Skins—" Vanya shouted, but McConnell pushed her away from him.

While the bear was crushing Koloff to death McConnell fell to his knees and proceeded to load the rifle Sun Rising had dropped.

By the time the bear was finished with Koloff, McConnell had loaded the rifle and had aimed it at the beast.

The bear stood its ground, confused for a moment. It wasn't quite sure which way to go.

McConnell held his fire, waiting for the bear to decide.

Seeing the bear hesitate, Sun Rising scooted on her hands and knees and grabbed the pistol, powder horn, and bag that McConnell had dropped and proceeded to load the pistol. She did it slowly, because she had never done it herself.

"Hey! Hey!" Vanya started to shout, attracting the bear's attention.

McConnell got to his feet, moved to his right, and shouted, "Hey you, over here!" causing the animal further confusion.

He knew that if they had enough guns the bear would be at their mercy. As it was, he had to make a perfect shot to kill it with the one ball he had.

"Hey!" Sun Rising shouted, pointing the pistol at the bear.

Still on his hind legs and standing nearly twelve feet high, the animal was a fearsome enough sight, but as he let out a roar of confusion and rage he made their blood run cold. Huge gobs of saliva dripped from its jaw onto the snow. Finally the animal settled on a direction. He came down off his hind legs and headed for Vanya, the only one of the three of them who was unarmed.

"Sun Rising, fire!" McConnell shouted.

Sun Rising extended the pistol, holding it in both hands, and fired. The ball struck the bear on the left rear hindquarter, but that didn't slow him.

Rather than being rooted to the spot by her fear, Vanya flew into motion. She ran to her right, causing the bear to veer.

McConnell was still trying to figure his perfect shot, and feared that he had let it get away while the bear was standing on its hind legs. Now he knew he had to fire or watch the bear dismember Vanya.

He fired just as the bear had lifted a paw and was bringing it down toward Vanya, who was again trying to duck away. The monster's huge claws caught in her clothing, throwing her to the ground.

McConnell's ball struck the animal high on its back,

almost on the back of the neck, where he had been aiming. The bear seemed to pause a moment, even seemed to peer over its shoulder at McConnell for a split second, and then turned its attention back to Vanya.

Knowing his gesture would be futile, McConnell reversed the rifle in his hands and charged.

Pike saw the fire of the camp and hoped he was making the right move. He also hoped that he had beaten Koloff back.

When he heard the sound of the bear's roar he knew that Koloff was the least of his worries.

He broke into a run, his rifle at the ready.

On the second blow to the bear's back the rifle stock shattered, and still the animal stalked Vanya, who was crawling backward, trying to get away. The beast seemed to be taking its time, knowing now that no one in camp could hurt it and that it had all the time in the world to take its vengeance for the death of its mate.

"Skins!" Sun Rising called.

He turned and saw that she had reloaded the pistol. She tossed it to him and he caught it. As he turned back to the bear he heard Vanya scream and the beast roar. With a swipe of its paw the snow turned red and McConnell fired . . .

Pike entered camp just as McConnell fired the pistol into the bear's back. He saw Vanya's blood on the snow and in an instant knew what had happened. Moving closer, he aimed the rifle and fired. His ball struck the beast on the side of the head, but the animal's skull was so thick that the ball glanced off, gouging skin as it continued across the top of the bear's head.

The animal roared in pain and jerked its head as blood poured down over its face from the scalp wound.

"Skins!" Pike shouted, and as McConnell turned toward him he tossed over his rifle. "Reload!"

"What are you going to do?"

"Distract him."

Pike didn't know if Vanya was still alive or not, but he couldn't take the chance that she wasn't. He took out his knife, rushed the bear, and launched himself in a dive that carried him onto the beast's back.

The stench of the animal was overwhelming, and Pike was surprised at how thick its fur was. He closed his left hand over the fur, taking a firm hold, and then brought his right arm around the monster's thick neck. He could see over the bear's shoulder that Vanya was still alive, her eyes fluttering, but she wasn't moving very much.

He lifted the knife, tightening his knees on the bear's back, and brought the blade down, driving it into the right shoulder. The roar of pain and rage was deafening. As he lifted the blade again, the animal's blood sprayed everywhere. Pike brought the knife down again, and then again . . .

He was hurting the beast, he knew, but the animal did not seem to be weakening. It did, however, turn its attention away from Vanya and start to circle, trying to get at whatever was causing it pain.

The bear turned and turned, blurring Pike's vision and making it hard for McConnell to take a shot without fear of hitting Pike.

Suddenly the bear drew up onto its hind legs, its

249

back to McConnell so he still couldn't shoot. Pike realized suddenly that if the bear fell onto its back it would crush him. How long would it be before the same thought occurred to the bear?

Realizing that he had done as much damage as he could, Pike decided to take a chance. He pulled with his left hand and dug in with his heels, trying to climb the beast's back a little higher. When he had the purchase he needed he brought the knife around, jammed it beneath the slathering jaws, and ripped it across the thick neck. He felt the knife bite and blood flow onto his hand.

The bear's reaction was so violent that Pike was thrown from its back. He flew through the air and landed hard on the snow, trying desperately to orient himself. He looked up and saw the bear flailing around the camp, knocking over tents, trampling the fire, running amok with no sense of direction, and all the while roaring and bleeding profusely from its slit throat.

Pike scrambled over to where Vanya lay and covered her with his body. The bear continued to stagger about, coming dangerously close to trampling them all and covering them in its blood. Sun Rising was darting about, trying to stay clear of the bear's path, and McConnell kept moving, trying to draw a bead for a killing shot.

Pike knew that eventually the bear would bleed to death, but before it did it might succeed in killing them all without even realizing it. A lot depended on McConnell's shot . . . Pike watched his friend and held his breath.

McConnell continued following the bear's progress, moving away when it came toward him and then trying again to draw down on it.

Finally Pike pushed himself off Vanya and cried,

"Damn it, Skins, take the shot!"

At that very moment McConnell found the shot he wanted and fired. The ball traveled true and struck the bear's head. This time, instead of glancing off the animal's skull it punched a hole through the bone and drove into the brain. When it struck the other side of the skull it flattened out and ricocheted back through the brain. When the bear struck the ground they all swore they felt the earth shiver. Then suddenly it was as quiet as . . . death . . .

Pike rose to his feet. He walked over to where McConnell was standing over the fallen animal.

"Nice shot," Pike said, "but what the hell took you so long?"

Epilogue

Only three of them remained when they rode back into Clark's Fork several days later. The last of the Russians, Vanya, had died the day after the bear attack. Her wounds had been too serious for her to survive the trip. They had carried her body with them, wrapped in a blanket, and when they were free of the snow they buried her. They scraped out a shallow grave for Leonid, but the bodies of Makarov and Koloff were left where they lay.

Upon arriving in Clark's Fork they went directly to Ted Clark's. His wife was the closest thing to a doctor the settlement had.

Pike had a drink and Sun Rising sat with him while Sky Woman looked McConnell over.

Ted Clark finally came out and joined them.

"The ride back aggravated the wound," he said. "There's some infection. Sky Woman says he'll have to stay off it for a while or he might lose the leg."

"Then he'll stay off it," Pike said. "We'll pitch a tent—"

"I've got an extra bed out back in a small storeroom. He can stay there."

"Thanks, Ted."

"Sky Woman will be able to look after him better

this way. Where are you gonna stay?"

"I'll pitch a tent outside the settlement."

"And Sun Rising?"

Pike looked at Sun Rising, then said to Clark, "She'll stay with me."

Over the next week Sun Rising cooked all Pike's meals and washed his clothes. It seemed to be an unspoken agreement between them. She had wanted to be with him ever since the first time they met, and although he had been attracted to her, she had been Walking Cat's woman at the time.

Now, nothing was standing in their way.

On the first night in the tent outside the settlement, they both knew what they wanted . . .

Sun Rising cooked him some dinner and they had eaten it together. After that Pike had gone to Clark's to look in on McConnell, who was asleep. Pike had a beer with Clark at the bar, then said good night and went back to the tent.

When he entered the tent he saw that she had laid out his blankets on the floor of the tent and was kneeling on them, waiting for him . . . naked.

By the light of the storm lamp he could see how beautiful she truly was. The light made secrets of some parts of her body, shrouding them in shadow. He quickly discarded his clothing and joined her, wanting to discover all those secrets . . . and more . . .

He used his hands and his mouth to explore her, and then she turned him over and mounted him, dangling her full breasts in his face. He squeezed them, sucking and biting the nipples as she rode him. Her breasts were large enough for him to push them together and suck both nipples at one time. She moaned when he did that, and it was the only sound she made the whole time. Even when he felt her body start to shudder, when she threw her head back and rode him wildly, and when he exploded inside of her, she never made another sound—not until she dropped down onto his chest exhausted, pressing her cheek to his chest.

Then she sighed.

At the end of the week they looked to everyone like a couple. If they were not married, then she was obviously his squaw.

On the seventh day Pike went to see McConnell and found him sitting up, his feet on the floor.

"Skins—"

"That's it, Pike," McConnell said, "I've had it. I'm ready to move on."

"So am I," Pike said. "What does Sky Woman say?"

"She says I shouldn't ride for another week," McConnell said. "I say I should. If you're not coming along, I'll go alone, but I'm ready to go."

"All right, all right," Pike said, "we'll go. I'll put together an outfit for us."

As Pike headed for the door McConnell said, "Hey, Pike?"

"What?"

"Shouldn't we . . . I don't know, try to contact somebody in the government? I mean, about Severance and Koloff?"

"Why?"

"Well . . . Koloff's country is gonna want to know what happened to him."

"Let them send someone up here to find out," Pike

said. "We didn't ask for any of this, and we didn't get paid what we were supposed to. We were almost killed more times than I can remember. No, Skins, I don't think we should try to contact anyone about any of this . . . ever."

McConnell stared at his friend, saw how serious he was, and said, "All right."

"Good."

"What about Sun Rising?" McConnell asked.

Pike looked away, then looked back at McConnell.

"She'll ride with us for a while."

McConnell studied Pike for a few moments, realized he was just as serious about this, and asked, "It's like that, is it?"

Pike nodded and said, "It's like that . . . for a while."